U0025480

Daisy Miller
Henry James
黛絲・米勒
原著 Henry James
改寫 Janet Olearski
譯者 安卡斯

For the Student

 Listen to the story and do some activities on your Audio CD.

 Talk about the story.

For the Teacher

Go to our Readers Resource site for information on using readers and downloadable Resource Sheets, photocopiable Worksheets, and Tapescripts. www.helblingreaders.com

For lots of great ideas on using Graded Readers consult Reading Matters, the Teacher's Guide to using Helbling Readers.

Structures

Modal verb would	Non-defining relative clauses
I'd love to . . .	Present perfect continuous
Future continuous	Used to / would
Present perfect future	Used to / used to doing
Reported speech / verbs / questions	Second conditional
Past perfect	Expressing wishes and regrets
Defining relative clauses	

Structures from other levels are also included.

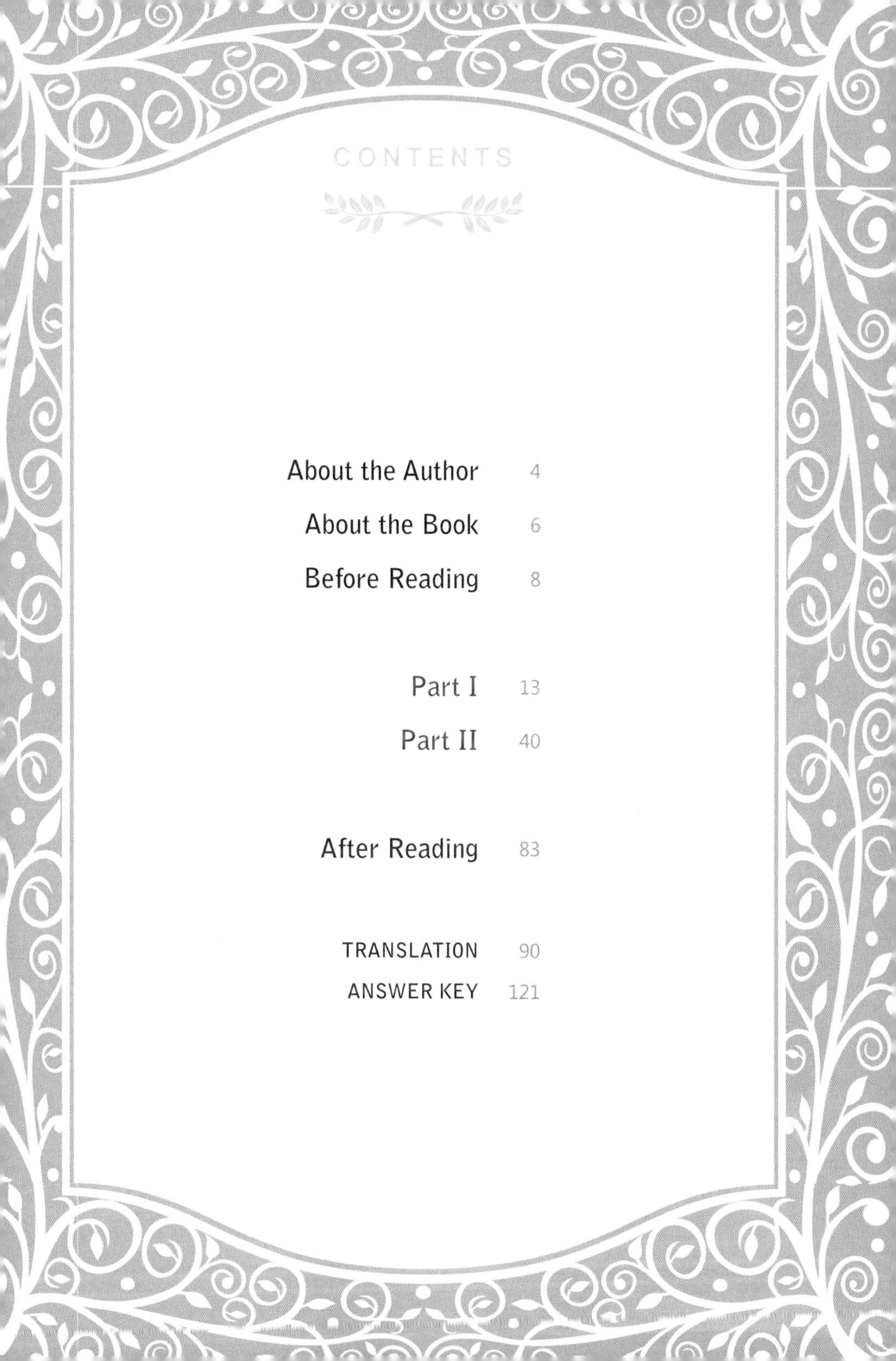

CONTENTS

About the Author 4

About the Book 6

Before Reading 8

Part I 13

Part II 40

After Reading 83

TRANSLATION 90

ANSWER KEY 121

About the Author

Henry James was born in New York in 1843 into a wealthy, intellectual family. He was named after his father, Henry James Senior, who was a well-known theologian[1]. When he was a child James travelled with his family back and forth between Europe and America, studying with tutors[2] for the time he was abroad[3].

James loved reading and could read fluently in French, Italian and German as well as his native English. In 1864, he anonymously[4] published his first short story, *A Tragedy of Error*, and from then on devoted[5] himself completely to literature.

Throughout his career, he wrote extensively[6], publishing books and articles in a variety of genres[7]: novels, short story collections, literary criticism, travel writing, biography and autobiography. In all, he wrote 22 novels, including two left unfinished at his death, and 112 stories, along with many plays[8] and essays[9].

James moved to Europe, settling permanently[10] in England in 1876. He lived there, first in London then in Rye, in Sussex. The outbreak[11] of World War I was a profound[12] shock for James, and in 1915, he became a British citizen to declare[13] his loyalty to his adopted country as well as to protest against America's refusal to enter the war on behalf of[14] Britain.

James died in London in 1916. He is considered by many writers and critics to be one of the greatest American authors and a number of his works have been made into successful films.

1 theologian [ˌθiəˋlodʒən] (n.) 神學家
2 tutor [ˋtjutɚ] (n.) 家庭教師
3 abroad [əˋbrɔd] (adv.) 在國外
4 anonymously [əˋnɑnəməslɪ] (adv.) 不具名地
5 devote [dɪˋvot] (v.) 致力於；獻身
6 extensively [ɪkˋstɛnsɪvlɪ] (adv.) 廣泛地
7 genre [ˋʒɑnrə] (n.)〔法〕文藝作品之類型
8 play [ple] (n.) 戲劇
9 essay [ˋɛse] (n.) 散文；隨筆
10 permanently [ˋpɝmənəntlɪ] (adv.) 永久地
11 outbreak [ˋaʊtˌbrek] (n.) 爆發
12 profound [prəˋfaʊnd] (a.) 深刻的
13 declare [dɪˋklɛr] (v.) 聲明
14 on behalf of 為了……的利益；代表

About the Book

Daisy Miller was first published in the June and July 1878 issues of *Cornhill* magazine, in Britain. It was an immediate success and gained James a reputation as an international author. The story is based on a piece of gossip that James recorded in his notebook.

It tells the story of a pretty young American girl, the Daisy Miller of the title, who is travelling around Europe with her mother and younger brother. Daisy meets a compatriot[1], Winterbourne, who is fascinated[2] by her open and friendly manner. However, Daisy's flirtatiousness[3] is frowned upon by the other expatriates[4] they meet and her lack of understanding of the unsaid rules of society ultimately[5] leads to tragedy.

The novella[6] explores a number of themes which James continued to explore in his later novels. It is one of his earliest treatments of the behavior of Americans abroad. In the years following the American Civil War[7] a new business class emerged and they soon were eager to further their children's education by taking them on the 'grand tour[8]' of Europe. James was drawn to the innocence and freshness of his compatriots while he also felt they were undereducated and provincial[9] compared to their European counterparts.

It also takes a look at another theme which is central to his work: that of the choice not to live one's life to the full. Throughout James' stories characters realize that what they were waiting for has passed them by and that they have wasted their whole lives, or parts of their lives thinking about it.

In *Daisy Miller* Winterbourne spends the entire novel trying to figure out Daisy, without ever understanding her or what she means to him. Many critics consider *Daisy Miller* to be a preface to James' later novel *Portrait of a Lady*.

1 compatriot [kəm`petrɪət] (n.) 同胞
2 fascinate [`fæsṇˏet] (v.) 迷住；使神魂顛倒
3 flirtatiousness [flɝ`teʃəsnɪs] (n.) 招蜂引蝶
4 expatriate [ɛks`petrɪˏet] (n.) 移居國外者
5 ultimately [`ʌltəmɪtlɪ] (adv.) 最終
6 novella [no`vɛlə] (n.) 中篇小說
7 Civil War 美國南北戰爭（1861–1865）
8 grand tour，指以前富家子弟接受學業的一個階段，他們會去歐洲大陸的主要國家和城市去旅遊，以增廣見聞，並接受教育
9 provincial [prə`vɪnʃəl] (a.) 粗野的；地方性的

Before Reading

1 Before you read the story, take a look at the pictures in the book. Write a list of ten words or expressions that you think will describe the story you are going to read. If possible, work with a partner and compare your lists.

2 The title of the story is *Daisy Miller*. What type of story do you think it will be and what do you think it will be about? Discuss the ideas below in groups of three or four.

- (a) A love story. A young woman called Daisy will fall in love and get married.
- (b) A tragedy. Daisy will make a serious mistake and someone will die as a result.
- (c) A mystery. Daisy will be involved in a series of mysterious events.

d. A family drama. There will be conflict between members of Daisy's family.

e. A travel story. Daisy will go on a long journey, and learn about life in the process.

Share your ideas with the rest of the class.

3 Look at this picture of Daisy Miller. What do you think she is like? Write down questions you would like to ask her. Ask and answer with a partner.

4 Imagine that you are the parents of a 16-year-old girl. What would you allow her to do and what would you not allow her to do? Write a list.

You are the parents of a 16-year-old girl.

Now imagine that you are the parents of a 16-year-old boy. Make a list of the things that you would allow him to do and the things you wouldn't allow him to do. Are your two lists the same or different?

You are the parents of a 16-year-old boy.

5 On a scale of 1 to 5 (1 = I don't agree at all; 5 = I agree entirely), how far do you agree with the following statements?

a Living for a long time in a foreign country helps you become more open-minded. 1 2 3 4 5

b When you live in a foreign country, you should behave just as you would in your own country. 1 2 3 4 5

c You should be careful not to offend people by doing things they don't approve of. 1 2 3 4 5

d If you love a person, their upbringing and social class are not important. 1 2 3 4 5

e Men can make friends with anyone they like, but women cannot. 1 2 3 4 5

1 establishment [ɪsˋtæblɪʃmənt] (n.) 建立
2 distinguished [dɪˋstɪŋgwɪʃt] (a.) 出色的
3 flitting [ˋflɪtɪŋ] (n.) 輕快地走動
4 rustling [ˋrʌsḷɪŋ] (n.) 沙沙作響
5 muslin [ˋmʌzlɪn] (n.) 平紋細布
6 frill [frɪl] (n.) 縐邊；荷葉邊
7 rattle [ˋrætḷ] (n.) 吵鬧聲
8 hight-pitched [ˋhaɪˋpɪtʃt] (n.) 聲調高的
9 inn [ɪn] (n.) 小旅館；小酒店
10 idly [ˋaɪdḷɪ] (adv.) 無所事事
11 steamer [ˋstimɚ] (n.) 汽船
12 residence [ˋrɛzədəns] (n.) 住所
13 at liberty 有空閒地

PART I

In the little town of Vevey, in Switzerland, there is a most comfortable hotel, which is seated upon the edge of a clear blue lake. The shore of the lake has a range of establishments[1] of this type. One of the hotels, however, is famous, being distinguished[2] from many of its neighbors by an air both of luxury and of maturity. In this region, in the month of June, American travelers are extremely numerous. There is a flitting[3] here and there of 'stylish' young girls, a rustling[4] of muslin[5] frills[6], a rattle[7] of dance music in the morning hours, a sound of high-pitched[8] voices at all times. You receive an impression of these things at the excellent inn[9] of the 'Trois Couronnes'.

I hardly know what was in the mind of a young American, who, two or three years ago, sat in the garden of the 'Trois Couronnes', looking about him, rather idly[10], at some of the graceful objects I have mentioned. He had come from Geneva the day before by the little steamer[11], to see his aunt, who was staying at the hotel—Geneva having been for a long time his place of residence[12]. But his aunt had a headache—his aunt had almost always a headache—and now she was closed in her room, so that he was at liberty[13] to wander about.

He was some seven-and-twenty years of age. His friends usually said that he was in Geneva 'studying'. Other people said that the reason he spent so much time in Geneva was that he was extremely devoted[1] to a lady who lived there—a foreign lady—a person older than himself. Very few Americans had ever seen this lady, about whom there were some curious stories. Winterbourne had gone to school and college in Geneva, and this had led to his forming a great many youthful friendships there. Many of these he had kept, and they were a source of great satisfaction to him.

After learning that his aunt was not feeling well, he had taken a walk about the town, and then he had come in to have breakfast. Now he was drinking a small cup of coffee at a little table in the garden. At last he finished his coffee and lit a cigarette. Soon a small boy of nine or ten came along the path. The child had a pale face, and was dressed in knickerbockers[2], with red stockings, which displayed[3] his poor little thin legs; he also wore a brilliant red cravat[4].

He carried a long alpenstock[5], the sharp point of which he thrust[6] into everything that he approached[7]—the flowerbeds, the garden benches, the trains[8] of the ladies' dresses. In front of Winterbourne he paused, looking at him with a pair of bright, penetrating[9] eyes.

1 devoted [dɪ`votɪd] (a.) 摯愛的
2 knickerbockers [`nɪkɚ͵bɑkɚz] (n.) 燈籠褲
3 display [dɪ`sple] (v.) 顯示
4 cravat [krə`væt] (n.) 領結；領巾
5 alpenstock [`ælpən͵stɑk] (n.) 鐵頭登山杖
6 thrust [θrʌst] (v.) 刺；插
7 approach [ə`protʃ] (v.) 接近

'Will you give me a lump[10] of sugar?' he asked in a hard little voice.

Winterbourne glanced[11] at the small table near him and saw that several pieces of sugar remained. 'Yes, you may take one,' he answered; 'but I don't think sugar is good for little boys.'

This little boy carefully selected three lumps of sugar, two of which he buried in the pocket of his knickerbockers, depositing[12] the other in his mouth. He tried to crack[13] it with his teeth.

'Oh, it's har-r-d!' he exclaimed, pronouncing the adjective in a peculiar manner.

Winterbourne had immediately perceived[14] that he might have the honor of claiming him as a fellow countryman. 'Take care you don't hurt your teeth,' he said, paternally[15].

'I haven't got any teeth to hurt. I have only got seven teeth. My mother said she'd slap[16] me if any more came out. It's the climate that makes them come out.'

Winterbourne was greatly amused[17]. 'If you eat three lumps of sugar, your mother will certainly slap you,' he said.

CHILDHOOD

- Think back to when you were a child. Did you have any habits that annoyed your parents or guardians? What did they say to you?

8 train [tren] (n.) 下襬；裙裾
9 penetrating [`pɛnə,tretɪŋ] (a.) 有穿透力的
10 lump [lʌmp] (n.) 塊
11 glance [glæns] (v.) 瞥
12 deposit [dɪ`pɑzɪt] (v.) 放置
13 crack [kræk] (v.) 使霹啪作響
14 perceive [pɚ`siv] (v.) 察覺
15 paternally [pə`tɝnəlɪ] (adv.) 父親般地
16 slap [slæp] (v.) 摑
17 amused [ə`mjuzd] (a.) 被逗樂的

'Here comes my sister!' cried the child.

Winterbourne looked along the path and saw a beautiful young lady advancing[1]. She was dressed in white muslin, with a hundred frills, and knots of pale-colored ribbon. She had no hat on, but she balanced in her hand a large parasol[2] and she was very pretty.

The little boy had now converted[3] his alpenstock into a vaulting[4] pole, with which he was springing[5] about in the gravel[6] and kicking up the dust.

'Randolph,' said the young lady, 'what *are* you doing?'

'I'm going up the Alps,' replied Randolph. 'This is the way!' And he gave another little jump, scattering[7] the pebbles[8] about Winterbourne's ears.

The young lady looked straight at her brother. 'Well, I guess you had better be quiet,' she simply observed[9].

Winterbourne got up and stepped slowly towards the young girl, throwing away his cigarette. 'This little boy and I have made acquaintance[10],' he said, with great politeness.

In Geneva, a young man was not at liberty to speak to a young unmarried lady except under certain conditions; but here at Vevey, what conditions could be better than these?—a pretty American girl coming and standing in front of you in a garden.

This pretty American girl, however, simply glanced at him; she then turned her head and looked over the parapet[11], at the lake and the opposite mountains. Winterbourne wondered whether he had gone too far, but he decided that he must advance farther, rather than retreat[12]. While he was thinking of something else to say, the young lady turned to the little boy again.

1. advance [əd`væns] (v.) 向前進
2. parasol [`pærə͵sɔl] (n.) 陽傘
3. convert [kən`vɝt] (v.) 變換
4. vaulting [`vɔltɪŋ] (a.) 跳躍用的
5. spring [sprɪŋ] (v.) 跳躍
6. gravel [`grævl̩] (n.) 小石；砂礫
7. scatter [`skætɚ] (v.) 散佈
8. pebble [`pɛbl̩] (n.) 小卵石
9. observe [əb`zɝv] (v.) 說；評論
10. acquaintance [ə`kwentəns] (n.) 相識
11. parapet [`pærəpɪt] (n.) 低矮的擋牆或欄杆
12. retreat [rɪ`trit] (v.) 撤退

'I should like to know where you got that pole,' she said.

'I bought it,' responded Randolph.

'You don't mean you're going to take it to Italy?'

'Yes, I *am* going to take it to Italy,' the child declared[1].

'Are you going to Italy?' Winterbourne inquired[2] in a tone of great respect.

The young lady glanced at him again. 'Yes, sir,' she replied.

'Are you going over the Simplon?' Winterbourne pursued[3], a little embarrassed.

'I don't know,' she said. 'I suppose it's some mountain. Randolph, what mountain are we going over?'

'I don't know,' said Randolph. 'I don't want to go to Italy. I want to go to America.'

'Oh, Italy is a beautiful place!' answered the young man.

TRAVEL

- Have you ever travelled abroad?
- What did you like about the places you visited?
- What did you miss about home?

The young lady inspected[4] her dress and smoothed her ribbons. Winterbourne was ceasing[5] to be embarrassed, for he had begun to notice that she was not at all embarrassed herself. There had not been the slightest change in her charming complexion[6]; she was evidently neither offended[7] nor flattered[8].

1 declare [dɪˋklɛr] (v.) 宣告；宣稱
2 inquire [ɪnˋkwaɪr] (v.) 訊問；查問
3 pursue [pɚˋsu] (v.) 追問
4 inspect [ɪnˋspɛkt] (v.) 檢查

If she looked another way when he spoke to her, and seemed not particularly to hear him, this was simply her manner. Yet, as he talked a little more and pointed out some of the objects of interest in the view, with which she appeared quite unacquainted, she gradually gave him more of the benefit of her glance; and then he saw that this glance was perfectly direct. The young girl's eyes were honest and fresh. They were wonderfully pretty eyes.

Winterbourne had a great relish[9] for feminine[10] beauty; he was addicted[11] to observing and analyzing it. He thought it very possible that Master Randolph's sister was a coquette[12]; he was sure she had a spirit of her own; but in her bright, sweet, superficial[13] little face there was no mockery[14], no irony.

Before long it became obvious that she was much disposed[15] towards conversation. She told him that they were going to Rome for the winter—she and her mother and Randolph. She told him she was from New York State—'if you know where that is.'

Winterbourne caught hold of her small brother and made him stand a few minutes by his side.

'Tell me your name, my boy,' he said.

'Randolph C. Miller,' said the boy sharply. 'And her name is Daisy Miller!' cried the child. 'But that isn't her real name. Her real name is Annie P. Miller.'

5 cease [sis] (v.) 停止
6 complexion [kəmˋplɛkʃən] (n.) 氣色
7 offend [əˋfɛnd] (v.) 冒犯
8 flatter [ˋflætɚ] (v.) 奉承
9 relish [ˋrɛlɪʃ] (n.) 愛好
10 feminine [ˋfɛmənɪn] (a.) 女性的
11 addicted [əˋdɪktɪd] (a.) 入了迷的
12 coquette [koˋkɛt] (n.) 賣弄風情的人
13 superficial [ˌsupɚˋfɪʃəl] (a.) 表面的
14 mockery [ˋmɑkərɪ] (n.) 嘲笑；嘲弄
15 disposed [dɪˋspozd] (a.) 打算做……的

8

'Ask him *his* name,' said his sister, indicating[1] Winterbourne.

But on this point Randolph seemed perfectly indifferent[2]; he continued to supply[3] information regarding his own family. 'My father's name is Ezra B. Miller,' he announced[4]. 'My father's in Schenectady. He's got a big business. My father's rich, you bet[5]!'

'Well!' exclaimed[6] Miss Miller, lowering her parasol and looking at the embroidered[7] border[8].

Winterbourne released[9] the child, who departed[10], dragging[11] his alpenstock along the path.

'He doesn't like Europe,' said the young girl. 'He wants to go back. Mother's going to get a teacher for him as soon as we get to Italy. Can you get good teachers in Italy?'

'Very good, I should think,' said Winterbourne.

'Or else she's going to find some school. He ought to learn some more. He's only nine. He's going to college.'

And in this way Miss Miller continued to converse[12] upon the affairs[13] of her family and upon other topics. She sat there with her extremely pretty hands folded in her lap[14], and with her pretty eyes now resting upon those of Winterbourne, now wandering over the garden, the people who passed by, and the beautiful view.

She talked to Winterbourne as if she had known him a long time. He found it very pleasant. It was many years since he had heard a young girl talk so much. She was very quiet; she sat in a charming, tranquil[15] attitude, but her lips and her eyes were constantly moving. She had a soft, slender[16], agreeable voice, and her tone was decidedly[17] sociable.

1 indicate [ˋɪndəˏket] (v.) 指出
2 indifferent [ɪnˋdɪfərənt] (a.) 不感興趣的
3 supply [səˋplaɪ] (v.) 提供
4 announce [əˋnaʊns] (v.) 聲稱
5 you bet 一點也沒錯
6 exclaim [ɪksˋklem] (v.) 大聲叫嚷
7 embroidered [ɪmˋbrɔɪdɚd] (a.) 繡花的
8 border [ˋbɔrdɚ] (n.) 邊緣
9 release [rɪˋlis] (v.) 放開
10 depart [dɪˋpɑrt] (v.) 離開
11 drag [dræg] (v.) 拖

She gave Winterbourne a history of her movements and intentions and those of her mother and brother, in Europe, and enumerated[18], in particular, the various hotels at which they had stopped. She declared that the hotels were very good, once you got used to their ways, and that Europe was perfectly sweet.

'The only thing I don't like,' she proceeded[19], 'is the society[20]. There isn't any society; or, if there is, I don't know where it keeps itself. Do you? I'm very fond of society, and I have always had a great deal of it. I don't mean only in Schenectady, but in New York. I used to go to New York every winter. In New York I had lots of society. I have more friends in New York than in Schenectady—more gentleman friends; and more young lady friends too.'

12 converse [kən`vɜs] (v.) 交談
13 affair [ə`fɛr] (n.) 事情
14 lap [læp] (n.) 膝部
15 tranquil [`træŋkwɪl] (a.) 平靜的
16 slender [`slɛndɚ] (a.) 細的
17 decidedly [dɪ`saɪdɪdlɪ] (adv.) 明確地
18 enumerate [ɪ`njuməˏret] (v.) 列舉
19 proceed [prə`sid] (v.) 繼續進行
20 society [sə`saɪətɪ] (n.) 社交界

She was looking at Winterbourne with all her prettiness in her lively eyes and in her light, slightly monotonous[1] smile. 'I have always had plenty of gentlemen's society.'

Poor Winterbourne was amused, perplexed[2], and decidedly charmed. He had never yet heard a young girl express herself in just this fashion. He felt that he had lived at Geneva so long that he had lost a great deal; he had become unaccustomed to the American tone.

Never, indeed, since he had grown old enough to appreciate[3] things, had he encountered[4] a young American girl of so pronounced a type as this. Certainly she was very charming, but how sociable! Was she simply a pretty girl from New York State? Were they all like that, the pretty girls who had a good deal of gentlemen's society? Or was she also a designing[5], an audacious[6], an unscrupulous[7] young person?

Winterbourne had lost his instinct[8] in this matter, and his reason could not help him. Miss Daisy Miller looked extremely innocent. Some people had told him that American girls were exceedingly[9] innocent; and others had told him that they were not.

He was inclined[10] to think Miss Daisy Miller was a flirt[11]—a pretty American flirt. He had never, as yet, had any relations with young ladies of this category. He had known, here in Europe, two or three women—persons older than Miss Daisy Miller, and provided, for respectability's sake, with husbands—who were great coquettes. They were dangerous, terrible women, with whom one's relations were liable to take a serious turn. But this young girl was not a coquette in that sense; she was very unsophisticated[12]; she was only a pretty American flirt.

'Have you been to that old castle?' asked the young girl, pointing with her parasol to the walls of the Chateau de Chillon.

'Yes, more than once,' said Winterbourne. 'You too, I suppose, have seen it?'

'No, we haven't been there. I want to go there very much indeed.'

'It's a very pretty excursion[13],' said Winterbourne. 'You can drive, you know, or you can go by the little steamer. I should think it might be arranged,' said Winterbourne. 'Couldn't you get someone to stay for the afternoon with Randolph?'

Miss Miller looked at him a moment, and then, very placidly[14], 'I wish *you* would stay with him!' she said.

Winterbourne hesitated[15] a moment. 'I should much rather go to Chillon with you.'

'With me?' asked the young girl with the same placidity[16].

'With your mother,' he answered very respectfully.

'Then we may arrange it. If Mother will stay with Randolph, I guess Eugenio will stay too.'

'Eugenio?' the young man inquired.

'Eugenio's our courier[17]. He doesn't like staying with Randolph, but I guess he'll stay with him if Mother does, and then we can go to the castle.'

1 monotonous [mə`nɑtənəs] (a.) 單調的；不變的
2 perplexed [pɚ`plɛkst] (a.) 困惑的
3 appreciate [ə`priʃɪˏet] (v.) 領會；察知
4 encounter [ɪn`kaʊntɚ] (v.) 偶遇
5 designing [dɪ`zaɪnɪŋ] (a.) 有預謀的
6 audacious [ɔ`deʃəs] (a.) 大膽無畏的
7 unscrupulous [ʌn`skrupjələs] (a.) 肆無忌憚的
8 instinct [`ɪnstɪŋkt] (n.) 本能
9 exceedingly [ɪk`sidɪŋlɪ] (adv.) 極度
10 inclined [ɪn`klaɪnd] (a.) 傾向的
11 flirt [flɝt] (n.) 調情者
12 unsophisticated [ˏʌnsə`fɪstɪˏketɪd] (a.) 不世故的
13 excursion [ɪk`skɝʒən] (n.) 短途旅行
14 placidly [`plæsɪdlɪ] (adv.) 平靜地
15 hesitate [`hɛzəˏtet] (v.) 猶豫
16 placidity [plə`sɪdətɪ] (n.) 平穩；沈著
17 courier [`kʊrɪɚ] (n.) 旅行時之從僕

Winterbourne reflected[1] for an instant—'we' could only mean Miss Daisy Miller and himself. This program seemed almost too delightful to believe; he felt as if he ought to kiss the young lady's hand, but at this moment another person, presumably[2] Eugenio, appeared.

A tall, handsome man, with a superb[3] moustache[4], wearing a velvet[5] morning coat and a brilliant watch chain, approached Miss Miller, looking sharply at her companion.

'Oh, Eugenio!' said Miss Miller with the friendliest accent[6].

Eugenio had looked at Winterbourne from head to foot; he now bowed gravely[7] to the young lady. 'I have the honor to inform mademoiselle[8] that luncheon[9] is upon the table.'

Miss Miller slowly rose. 'See here, Eugenio!' she said; 'I'm going to that old castle, anyway.'

'To the Chateau de Chillon, mademoiselle?' the courier inquired. 'Mademoiselle has made arrangements?' he added in a tone which struck Winterbourne as very rude.

The young girl turned to Winterbourne, blushing[10] a little. 'You won't back out[11]?' she said.

'I shall not be happy till we go!' he protested.

'And you are staying in this hotel?' she went on. 'Are you really an American?'

The courier stood looking at Winterbourne offensively[12]. Winterbourne thought his manner of looking at Miss Miller showed disapproval[13], as she 'picked up[14]' acquaintances.

1 reflect [rɪ`flɛkt] (v.) 思考
2 presumably [prɪ`zuməblɪ] (adv.) 據推測；大概
3 superb [sʊ`pɝb] (a.) 極好的
4 moustache [məs`tæʃ] (n.) 八字鬍
5 velvet [`vɛlvɪt] (a.) 天鵝絨的
6 accent [`æksɛnt] (n.) 腔調
7 gravely [`grevlɪ] (adv.) 莊重地
8 mademoiselle [ˌmædəmə`zɛl] (n.) 小姐
9 luncheon [`lʌntʃən] (n.) 午餐
10 blush [blʌʃ] (v.) 臉紅
11 back out 退出（計畫等）
12 offensively [ə`fɛnsɪvlɪ] (adv.) 令人不愉快地
13 disapproval [ˌdɪsə`pruvl̩] (n.) 不贊成
14 pick up 把男友；把女友

13

'I shall have the honor of presenting to you a person who will tell you all about me,' he said, smiling and referring to[1] his aunt.

She gave him a smile and turned away. She put up her parasol and walked back to the inn beside Eugenio.

Winterbourne stood looking after her; and as she moved away, said to himself that she appeared as elegant[2] as a princess.

DAISY MILLER

- What does Winterbourne think of Daisy Miller?

He had, however, promised to do more than proved[3] possible, in promising to present his aunt, Mrs Costello, to Miss Daisy Miller. In his aunt's apartment, after making the proper inquiries in regard to her health, he asked if she had observed in the hotel an American family—a mamma, a daughter, and a little boy.

'And a courier?' said Mrs Costello. 'Oh yes, I have observed them, seen them, heard them, and kept out of their way.'

Mrs Costello was a widow[4] with a fortune; a person of much distinction[5]. She had two sons married in New York and another who was now in Europe. This young man was amusing himself in Hamburg, and rarely visited any particular city at the moment selected by his mother for her own appearance there.

1 refer to 提及
2 elegant [ˋɛləgənt] (a.) 優雅的
3 prove [pruv] (v.) 證明
4 widow [ˋwɪdo] (n.) 寡婦
5 distinction [dɪˋstɪŋkʃən] (n.) 榮譽
6 attentive [əˋtɛntɪv] (a.) 留意的

Her nephew, who had come up to Vevey especially to see her, was therefore more attentive[6] than those who, as she said, were nearer to her. Mrs Costello had not seen him for many years, and she was greatly pleased with him.

He immediately noted, from her tone, that Miss Daisy Miller's place in the social scale was low.

'I am afraid you don't approve[7] of them,' he said.

'They are very common,' Mrs Costello declared.

'Ah, you don't accept them?' said the young man.

'I can't, my dear Frederick. I would if I could, but I can't.'

'The young girl is very pretty,' said Winterbourne.

'Of course she's pretty. But she is very common. She has that charming look that they all have,' his aunt resumed, 'and she dresses perfectly. I can't think where they get their taste. They treat the courier like a familiar friend—like a gentleman. I shouldn't wonder if he dines[8] with them. Very likely they have never seen a man with such good manners, such fine clothes, so like a gentleman. He probably corresponds[9] to the young lady's idea of a count[10]. He sits with them in the garden in the evening. I think he smokes.'

Winterbourne listened with interest to these disclosures[11]; they helped him to make up his mind about Miss Daisy. Evidently[12] she was rather wild.

'Well,' he said, 'I am not a courier, and yet she was very charming to me.'

7 approve [ə`pruv] (v.) 贊成
8 dine [daɪn] (v.) 用餐
9 correspond [ˌkɔrɪ`spɑnd] (v.) 符合
10 count [kaʊnt] (n.) 伯爵
11 disclosure [dɪs`kloʒɚ] (n.) 透露
12 evidently [`ɛvədəntlɪ] (adv.) 顯然地

'You had better have said at first,' said Mrs Costello with dignity[1], 'that you had made her acquaintance.'

'We simply met in the garden, and we talked a bit. I said I should take the liberty of introducing her to my admirable aunt.'

'I am much obliged[2] to you.'

'It was to guarantee[3] my respectability[4],' said Winterbourne.

'And who is to guarantee hers?'

'Ah, you are cruel!' said the young man. 'She's a very nice young girl. She is completely uncultivated[5],' Winterbourne went on. 'But she is wonderfully pretty, and, in short, she is very nice. I am going to take her to the Chateau de Chillon.'

'How long had you known her, may I ask, when this interesting project was formed?'

'I have known her half an hour!' said Winterbourne, smiling.

'Dear me!' cried Mrs Costello. 'What a dreadful girl! You have lived too long out of the country. You will be sure to make some great mistake. You are too innocent.'

'My dear aunt, I am not so innocent,' said Winterbourne, smiling and curling[6] his moustache.

'You are guilty too, then!'

Winterbourne continued to curl his moustache meditatively[7].

'You won't let the poor girl know you then?' he asked.

'Is it true that she is going to the Chateau de Chillon with you?'

'I think that she fully intends it.'

1 dignity [ˋdɪgnətɪ] (n.) 尊嚴；尊貴
2 obliged [əˋblaɪdʒɪd] (a.) 使感激的
3 guarantee [ˏgærənˋti] (v.) 保證
4 respectability [rɪˏspɛktəˋbɪlətɪ] (n.) 可尊敬；體面
5 uncultivated [ʌnˋkʌltəˏvetɪd] (a.) 無教養的
6 curl [kɝl] (v.) 捲曲
7 meditatively [ˋmɛdəˏtetɪvlɪ] (adv.) 沈思地

'Then, my dear Frederick,' said Mrs Costello, 'I must decline[8] the honor of her acquaintance. I am an old woman, but I am not too old, thank Heaven, to be shocked!'

'But don't they all do these things—the young girls in America?' Winterbourne inquired.

Mrs Costello stared a moment. 'I should like to see my granddaughters do them!' she declared grimly[9].

Though he was impatient[10] to see Daisy, he hardly knew what he should say to her about his aunt's refusal[11] to become acquainted with her. He found her that evening in the garden, wandering about in the warm starlight. It was ten o'clock. Miss Daisy Miller seemed very glad to see him.

'Have you been all alone?' he asked.

'I have been walking round with Mother. But Mother gets tired walking round,' she answered. 'She doesn't like to go to bed,' said the young girl. 'She doesn't sleep—not three hours. She's dreadfully nervous.'

Winterbourne strolled[12] about with the young girl for some time without meeting her mother.

'I have been looking round for that lady you want to introduce me to,' his companion resumed. 'She's your aunt.'

She had heard all about Mrs Costello from the chambermaid[13]. She was very quiet, she spoke to no one, and she never dined at the table d'hôte[14]. Every two days she had a headache.

8 decline [dɪˋklaɪn] (v.) 婉拒；謝絕
9 grimly [ˋgrɪmlɪ] (ad.) 嚴厲地
10 impatient [ɪmˋpeʃənt] (a.) 急盼的
11 refusal [rɪˋfjuzḷ] (n.) 拒絕
12 stroll [strol] (v.) 散步
13 chambermaid [ˋtʃembɚ͵med] (n.) 旅館房間部的女服務生
14 table d'hôte 旅館的餐廳

(17) 'I think that's a lovely description[1], headache and all!' said Miss Daisy, chattering along in her thin, gay[2] voice. 'I want to know her ever so much. I know I should like her. She would be very exclusive[3]. I'm dying to be exclusive myself. Well, we *are* exclusive, Mother and I. We don't speak to everyone—or they don't speak to us. I suppose it's about the same thing. Anyway, I shall be ever so glad to know your aunt.'

Winterbourne was embarrassed. 'She would be most happy,' he said; 'but I am afraid those headaches will interfere[4].'

EXCUSES

- Have you ever made an excuse when you couldn't or didn't want to do something? Why did you make it? Discuss with a partner.

1 description [dɪ`skrɪpʃən] (n.) 描繪
2 gay [ge] (a.) 快樂的；爽朗的
3 exclusive [ɪk`sklusɪv] (a.) 限制社交往來的
4 interfere [ˌɪntɚ`fɪr] (v.) 妨礙
5 sympathetically [ˌsɪmpə`θɛtɪklɪ] (adv.) 同情地
6 visible [`vɪzəbḷ] (a.) 可見的

The young girl looked at him through the dusk. 'But I suppose she doesn't have a headache every day,' she said sympathetically[5].

Winterbourne was silent a moment. 'She tells me she does,' he answered at last, not knowing what to say.

Miss Daisy Miller stopped and stood looking at him. Her prettiness was still visible[6] in the darkness; she was opening and closing her enormous[7] fan.

'She doesn't want to know me!' she said suddenly. 'Why don't you say so? You needn't be afraid.' And she gave a little laugh.

Winterbourne thought there was a tremor[8] in her voice; he was touched[9] by it.

'My dear young lady,' he protested, 'she knows no one. It's her bad health.'

The young lady, resuming her walk, gave an exclamation[10] in quite another tone. 'Well, here's Mother! I guess she hasn't got Randolph to go to bed.'

7 enormous [ɪˋnɔrməs] (a.) 巨大的
8 tremor [ˋtrɛmɚ] (n.) 顫抖
9 touched [tʌtʃt] (a.) 受感動的
10 exclamation [ˌɛkskləˋmeʃən] (n.) 叫喊

The figure[1] of a lady appeared at a distance, very indistinct[2] in the darkness, and advancing with a slow movement.

'I am afraid your mother doesn't see you,' said Winterbourne.

'She won't come here because she sees you.'

'Ah, then,' said Winterbourne, 'I had better leave you. I'm afraid your mother doesn't approve of my walking with you.'

Miss Miller gave him a serious glance. 'Mother doesn't like any of my gentlemen friends. She always makes a fuss[3] if I introduce a gentleman. But I *do* introduce them—almost always.'

By this time they had come up to Mrs Miller, who, as they drew near, walked to the parapet of the garden and leaned upon it, looking intently at the lake and turning her back to them.

'Mother!' said the young girl in a tone of decision.

The elder lady turned round.

'Mr Winterbourne,' said Miss Daisy Miller, introducing the young man very frankly[4] and prettily.

'Common,' she was, as Mrs Costello had said; yet it was a wonder to Winterbourne that, with her commonness, she had a singularly[5] delicate[6] grace.

Her mother was a small person, with a wandering eye, a very small nose, and a large forehead, decorated with frizzled[7] hair. Like her daughter, Mrs Miller was dressed with extreme elegance; she had enormous diamonds in her ears. She gave Winterbourne no greeting—she certainly was not looking at him.

1 figure [ˋfɪgjɚ] (n.) 體形
2 indistinct [ˏɪndɪˋstɪŋkt] (a.) 模糊的
3 fuss [fʌs] (n.) 大驚小怪
4 frankly [ˋfræŋklɪ] (adv.) 坦白地
5 singularly [ˋsɪŋgjələlɪ] (adv.) 格外地

'I was telling Mr Winterbourne about Randolph,' the young girl went on.

'Oh, yes!' said Winterbourne; 'I have the pleasure of knowing your son.'

'I think Randolph's real tiresome[8],' Daisy pursued.

'Well, Daisy Miller,' said the elder lady, 'I shouldn't think you'd want to talk against your own brother!'

'Well, he wouldn't go to that castle,' said the young girl. 'I'm going there with Mr Winterbourne.'

To this announcement, Daisy's mamma offered no response. Winterbourne took for granted[9] that she deeply disapproved of the projected excursion; but he said to himself that she was a simple, easily managed person, and that a few deferential[10] protestations[11] would take the edge from her displeasure.

'Yes,' he began, 'your daughter has kindly allowed me the honor of being her guide.'

'We've been thinking ever so much about going,' she pursued; 'but it seems as if we couldn't. Of course Daisy—she wants to go round. We visited several castles in England,' she added.

'Ah yes! In England there are beautiful castles,' said Winterbourne. 'But Chillon, here, is very well worth seeing.'

'Well, if Daisy feels up to it –' said Mrs Miller.

'Oh, I think she'll enjoy it!' Winterbourne declared. 'You are not disposed[12], madam,' he inquired, 'to undertake[13] it yourself?'

6 delicate [ˋdɛləkət] (a.) 嬌貴的
7 frizzled [ˋfrɪzḷd] (a.) 鬈髮的
8 tiresome [ˋtaɪrsəm] (a.) 令人厭倦的
9 take for granted 視為理所當然
10 deferential [ˌdɛfəˋrɛnʃəl] (a.) 恭敬的
11 protestation [ˌprɑtəsˋteʃən] (n.) 抗議
12 disposed [dɪˋspozd] (a.) 打算做的
13 undertake [ˌʌndɚˋtek] (v.) 著手做

'Yes, it would be lovely!' said Daisy. But she made no movement to accompany him.

'I should think you had better find out what time it is,' said her mother.

'It is eleven o'clock, madam,' said a voice, with a foreign accent, out of the neighboring darkness.

'Oh, Eugenio,' said Daisy, 'I am going out in a boat!'

Eugenio bowed. 'At eleven o'clock, mademoiselle?'

'I am going with Mr Winterbourne—this very minute[1]'

'Do tell her she can't,' said Mrs Miller to the courier.

'I think you had better not go out in a boat, mademoiselle,' Eugenio declared.

'I suppose you don't think it's proper[2]!' Daisy exclaimed. 'Eugenio doesn't think anything's proper.'

'Does mademoiselle propose to go alone?' asked Eugenio of Mrs Miller.

'Oh, no; with this gentleman!' answered Daisy's mamma.

The courier looked for a moment at Winterbourne and then, solemnly[3], with a bow, 'As mademoiselle pleases!' he said.

'Oh, I hoped you would make a fuss!' said Daisy. 'I don't care to go now. That's all I want—a little fuss!' And the young girl began to laugh again.

'Mr Randolph has gone to bed!' the courier announced coldly.

'Oh, Daisy, now we can go!' said Mrs Miller.

1 this very moment 此時此刻
2 proper [ˋprɑpɚ] (a.) 恰當的
3 solemnly [ˋsɑləmlɪ] (adv.) 嚴肅地
4 fan [fæn] (v.) 用扇子搧
5 puzzled [ˋpʌzḷd] (a.) 困惑的
6 smartly [ˋsmɑrtlɪ] (adv.) 伶俐地

Daisy turned away from Winterbourne, looking at him, smiling and fanning[4] herself. 'Good night,' she said; 'I hope you are disappointed, or disgusted, or something!'

He looked at her, taking the hand she offered him. 'I am puzzled[5],' he answered.

'Well, I hope it won't keep you awake!' she said very smartly[6]; and, under the escort[7] of the lucky Eugenio, the two ladies passed towards the house.

Winterbourne stood looking after them; he was indeed puzzled.

Two days afterward he went with her to the Castle of Chillon. He waited for her in the large hall of the hotel, where the couriers, the servants, the foreign tourists, were lounging[8] about and staring. It was not the place he should have chosen, but she had decided upon it.

She came tripping[9] downstairs, buttoning her long gloves, squeezing[10] her folded parasol against her pretty figure, dressed in an elegant travelling costume[11].

Winterbourne was a man of imagination and as he looked at her dress and, on the great staircase, her little rapid step, he felt as if there were something romantic happening. He could have believed he was going to elope[12] with her.

He passed out with her among all the idle people that were assembled[13] there; they were all looking at her very hard; she had begun to chatter[14] as soon as she joined him.

7 escort [ˋɛskɔrt] (n.) 護送
8 lounge [laʊndʒ] (v.) 靠；躺；閒蕩
9 trip [trɪp] (v.) 輕快地走
10 squeeze [skwiz] (v.) 擠；緊握
11 costume [ˋkɑstjum] (n.) 服裝
12 elope [ɪˋlop] (v.) 私奔
13 assemble [əˋsɛmbḷ] (v.) 集合
14 chatter [ˋtʃætɚ] (v.) 喋喋不休

She expressed a lively wish to go to Chillon in the little steamer; she declared that she had a passion[1] for steamboats. There was always such a lovely breeze[2] upon the water, and you saw such a lot of people.

The voyage[3] was not long, but Winterbourne's companion found time to say a great many things. People continued to look at her a great deal, and Winterbourne took much satisfaction in his pretty companion's distinguished air. He had been a little afraid that she would talk loudly, laugh too much. But he quite forgot his fears; he sat smiling, with his eyes upon her face, while, she made a great number of original remarks[4]. He had agreed to the idea that she was 'common'; but was she, or was he simply getting used to her commonness?

1 passion [ˋpæʃən] (n.) 熱情
2 breeze [briz] (n.) 微風
3 voyage [ˋvɔɪɪdʒ] (n.) 航海；航行
4 remark [rɪˋmark] (n.) 評論
5 vaulted [ˋvɔltɪd] (a.) 拱形的
6 chamber [ˋtʃembɚ] (n.) 室；房間
7 corkscrew [ˋkɔrk͵skru] (a.) 螺旋狀的
8 shudder [ˋʃʌdɚ] (n.) 戰慄

23

In the castle, Daisy tripped about the vaulted[5] chambers[6], rustled her skirts in the corkscrew[7] staircases, flirted back with a pretty little cry and a shudder[8] from the edge of the oubliettes[9], and turned a well-shaped ear to everything that Winterbourne told her about the place.

They had the good fortune to walk about without other company than that of the custodian[10]; and Winterbourne arranged with him that they should not be hurried. The custodian interpreted the arrangement generously—Winterbourne, on his side, had been generous—and left them quite to themselves.

Miss Miller found a great many reasons for asking Winterbourne sudden questions about himself—his family, his previous history, his tastes, his habits, his intentions. Of her own tastes, habits, and intentions Miss Miller was prepared to give the most definite[11], and indeed the most favorable account.

9 oubliette [͵ublɪ`ɛt] (n.) 地牢
10 custodian [kʌs`todɪən] (n.) 管理人
11 definite [`dɛfənɪt] (a.) 明確的

Daisy went on to say that she wished Winterbourne would travel with them. Winterbourne said that nothing could possibly please him so much, but that he unfortunately had other occupations [1].

'What do you mean?' said Miss Daisy, 'You are not in business.'

The young man admitted that he was not in business; but he had engagements [2] which would force him to go back to Geneva.

'Well, Mr Winterbourne,' said Daisy, 'I think you're horrid [3]!'

'Oh, don't say such dreadful [4] things!' said Winterbourne.

'I have half a mind to leave you here and go straight back to the hotel alone.' And for the next ten minutes she did nothing but call him horrid.

Poor Winterbourne was bewildered [5]; no young lady had ever been so agitated [6] by his movements. His companion, after this, opened fire upon the mysterious lady in Geneva whom she claimed [7] that he was hurrying back to see.

How did Miss Daisy Miller know that there was a charmer [8] in Geneva? Winterbourne, who denied the existence of such a person, was quite unable to discover. She seemed to him an extraordinary [9] mixture of innocence and crudity [10].

1 occupation [ˌɑkjəˋpeʃən] (n.) 職業
2 engagement [ɪnˋgedʒmənt] (n.) 約會
3 horrid [ˋhɔrɪd] (a.) 可怕的
4 dreadful [ˋdrɛdfəl] (a.) 可怕的
5 bewildered [bɪˋwɪldɚd] (a.) 困惑的
6 agitated [ˋædʒəˌtetɪd] (a.) 激動的
7 claim [klem] (v.) 斷言
8 charmer [ˋtʃɑrmɚ] (n.) 有魅力的人

'Does she never allow you more than three days at a time?' asked Daisy ironically[11]. 'I suppose, if you stay another day, she'll come after you in the boat.'

At last, she told him she would stop 'teasing[12]' him if he would promise her solemnly to come down to Rome in the winter.

'That's not a difficult promise to make,' said Winterbourne. 'My aunt has taken an apartment in Rome for the winter and has already asked me to come and see her.'

'I don't want you to come for your aunt,' said Daisy; 'I want you to come for me.'

He declared that he would certainly come. After this Daisy stopped teasing. Winterbourne took a carriage[13], and they drove back to Vevey in the dusk[14].

In the evening Winterbourne mentioned to Mrs Costello that he had spent the afternoon at Chillon with Miss Daisy Miller.

'She went with you all alone?'

'All alone.'

Mrs Costello sniffed[15] a little at her smelling bottle[16]. 'And that,' she exclaimed, 'is the young person whom you wanted me to know!'

9 extraordinary [ɪk`strɔrdn̩ˏɛrɪ] (a.) 特別的
10 crudity [`krudətɪ] (n.) 粗魯的行動
11 ironically [aɪ`rɑnɪklɪ] (adv.) 諷刺地
12 tease [tiz] (v.) 戲弄；取笑
13 carriage [`kærɪdʒ] (n.) 馬車
14 dusk [dʌsk] (n.) 黃昏
15 sniff [snɪf] (v.) 嗅；聞
16 smelling bottle 嗅鹽瓶（提神用）

PART II

Winterbourne, who had returned to Geneva the day after his excursion to Chillon, went to Rome towards the end of January. His aunt had been there for several weeks, and he had received a couple of letters from her.

'Those people you were so devoted to last summer at Vevey have turned up here, courier and all,' she wrote. 'They seem to have made several acquaintances. The young lady, however, is very intimate[1] with some third-rate[2] Italians, with whom she associates[3] in a way that makes much talk.'

Winterbourne, on arriving in Rome, would have discovered Mrs Miller's address and he would have gone to pay his compliments[4] to Miss Daisy.

'After what happened at Vevey, I may certainly call upon[5] them,' he said to Mrs Costello.

'If, after what happens—at Vevey and everywhere—you desire to keep up the acquaintance, you are very welcome. Of course a man may know everyone. Men are welcome to the privilege[6]!'

MEN AND WOMEN

- **Do you think society expects women to behave in a different way to men?**

'Pray what happens—here, for instance?' Winterbourne demanded.

'The girl goes about alone with her foreigners. As to what happens further, you must apply[7] elsewhere for information. She has picked up half a dozen of the regular Roman fortune hunters, and she takes them about to people's houses. When she comes to a party she brings with her a gentleman with a good deal of manner and a wonderful moustache.'

'And where is the mother?'

'I haven't the least idea. They are very dreadful people.'

Winterbourne meditated[8] a moment. 'They are very ignorant[9]—very innocent—but they are not bad.'

'They are hopelessly vulgar[10],' said Mrs Costello. 'Whether or not being hopelessly vulgar is being 'bad' is a question for philosophers. They are bad enough to dislike, at any rate; and for this short life that is quite enough.'

1. intimate [ˋɪntəmɪt] (a.) 親密的
2. third-rate [ˋθɝdˋret] (a.) 下等的
3. associate [əˋsoʃɪ,et] (v.) 使有聯繫
4. compliment [ˋkɑmpləmənt] (n.) 讚美的話；恭維
5. call upon 登門拜訪
6. privilege [ˋprɪvḷɪdʒ] (n.) 特權；優待
7. apply [əˋplaɪ] (v.) 請求；申請
8. meditate [ˋmɛdə,tet] (v.) 沈思
9. ignorant [ˋɪgnərənt] (a.) 無知的
10. vulgar [ˋvʌlgɚ] (a.) 粗俗的

The news that Daisy Miller was surrounded[1] by half a dozen wonderful moustaches checked[2] Winterbourne's impulse[3] to go at once to see her. He was annoyed at hearing of a state of affairs so little in harmony with an image that had lately flitted[4] in and out of his own meditations; the image of a very pretty girl looking out of an old Roman window and asking herself urgently when Mr Winterbourne would arrive.

He determined to wait a little before reminding Miss Miller of his claims to her attention, and he went to call upon other friends.

One of these was Mrs Walker, an American lady who had spent several winters in Geneva, where she had placed her children at school. She was a very accomplished[5] woman, and she lived in the Via Gregoriana. Winterbourne found her in a little red drawing room[6], filled with southern sunshine. He had not been there ten minutes when the servant came in, announcing 'Madame Mila!'

This announcement was soon followed by the entrance[7] of little Randolph Miller, who stopped in the middle of the room and stood staring at Winterbourne. An instant later his pretty sister entered; and then, after a considerable[8] interval[9], Mrs Miller slowly advanced.

'I know you!' said Randolph.

'I'm sure you know a great many things,' exclaimed Winterbourne, taking him by the hand. 'How is your education coming on?'

1 surround [səˋraund] (v.) 圍繞
2 check [tʃɛk] (v.) 停止；抑制
3 impulse [ˋɪmpʌls] (n.) 衝動
4 flit [flɪt] (v.) 輕快地移動
5 accomplished [əˋkɑmplɪʃt] (a.) 善於社交的
6 drawing room 會客室；客廳
7 entrance [ˋɛntrəns] (n.) 進入；登場
8 considerable [kənˋsɪdərəbḷ] (a.) 可觀的
9 interval [ˋɪntɚvḷ] (n.) 間隔

Daisy was exchanging greetings very prettily with her hostess, but when she heard Winterbourne's voice she quickly turned her head.

'Well, I declare[1]!' she said.

'I told you I should come, you know,' Winterbourne rejoined[2], smiling.

'You might have come to see me!' said Daisy.

'I arrived only yesterday.'

'I don't believe that!' the young girl declared.

Winterbourne turned with a protesting smile to her mother, but this lady evaded[3] his glance. Daisy had entered upon a lively conversation with her hostess; Winterbourne judged it becoming to address a few words to her mother.

'I hope you have been well since we parted at Vevey,' he said.

Mrs Miller now certainly looked at him. 'Not very well, sir,' she answered.

'She's got dyspepsia[4],' said Randolph. 'I've got it too. Father's got it. I've got it most!'

This announcement, instead of embarrassing Mrs Miller, seemed to relieve[5] her. 'I suffer from the liver,' she said. 'I think it's this climate.'

Winterbourne had a good deal of gossip[6] with Mrs Miller, during which Daisy chattered continually to her hostess. The young man asked Mrs Miller how she liked Rome.

'Well, I must say I am disappointed,' she answered. 'We had heard so much about it; I suppose we had heard too much. We had been led to expect something different.'

'Ah, wait a little, and you will become very fond of it,' said Winterbourne.

'I hate it worse and worse every day!' cried Randolph.

'But we have seen places,' resumed his mother, 'that I should put a long way before Rome.'

And in reply to Winterbourne's interrogation[7], 'Zurich is lovely; and we hadn't heard half so much about it.'

Winterbourne expressed the hope that her daughter at least found some gratification[8] in Rome, and she declared that Daisy was quite carried away[9].

'It's on account of[10] the society—the society's splendid[11]. She has made a great number of acquaintances. I must say they have been very sociable; they have taken her right in. And then she knows a great many gentlemen. Oh, she thinks there's nothing like Rome. Of course, it's a great deal pleasanter for a young lady if she knows plenty of gentlemen.'

By this time Daisy had turned her attention again to Winterbourne. 'I've been telling Mrs Walker how mean[12] you were!' the young girl announced.

'And what is the evidence[13] you have offered?' asked Winterbourne.

'Why, you were awfully[14] mean at Vevey,' said Daisy. 'You wouldn't stay there when I asked you.'

1 I declare! 我真驚訝！
2 rejoin [riˋdʒɔɪn] (v.) 回答；反駁
3 evade [ɪˋved] (v.) 避開
4 dyspepsia [dɪˋspɛpʃə] (n.) 消化不良
5 relieve [rɪˋliv] (v.) 使放心
6 gossip [ˋgɑsəp] (n.) 閒話
7 interrogation [ɪnˏtɛrəˋgeʃən] (n.) 訊問；審問
8 gratification [ˏgrætəfəˋkeʃən] (n.) 滿足
9 be carried away 入迷
10 on account of 由於
11 splendid [ˋsplɛndɪd] (a.) 光彩的
12 mean [min] (a.) 卑鄙的
13 evidence [ˋɛvədəns] (n.) 證據
14 awfully [ˋɔfʊlɪ] (adv.) 非常地

'My dearest young lady,' cried Winterbourne, with eloquence[1], 'have I come all the way to Rome to be criticized[2] by you?'

'Well, I don't know,' said Daisy, touching Mrs Walker's ribbons. 'Mrs Walker, I want to tell you something. You know I'm coming to your party.'

'I am delighted to hear it.'

'I've got a lovely dress!'

'I am very sure of that.'

'But I want to ask a favor—permission[3] to bring a friend.'

'I shall be happy to see any of your friends,' said Mrs Walker, turning with a smile to Mrs Miller.

'Oh, they are not my friends,' answered Daisy's mamma.

'It's an intimate friend of mine—Mr Giovanelli,' said Daisy without a tremor in her clear little voice.

Mrs Walker was silent a moment; she gave a rapid glance at Winterbourne. 'I shall be glad to see Mr Giovanelli,' she then said.

'He's an Italian. He's a great friend of mine; he's the handsomest man in the world—except Mr Winterbourne! He knows plenty of Italians, but he wants to know some Americans. He's tremendously[4] clever. He's perfectly lovely!'

It was settled that this brilliant personage[5] should be brought to Mrs Walker's party, and then Mrs Miller prepared to take her leave. 'I guess we'll go back to the hotel,' she said.

'You may go back to the hotel, Mother, but I'm going to take a walk,' said Daisy.

'She's going to walk with Mr Giovanelli,' Randolph proclaimed[6].

'Alone, my dear—at this hour?' Mrs Walker asked. 'I don't think it's safe, my dear.'

Daisy bent over and kissed her hostess. 'Mrs Walker, you are too perfect,' she said. 'I'm not going alone; I am going to meet a friend.'

'Is it Mr Giovanelli?' asked the hostess.

Winterbourne was watching the young girl; at this question his attention quickened. She stood there, smiling and smoothing her bonnet[7] ribbons; she glanced at Winterbourne, and answered, without a shade of hesitation, 'Mr Giovanelli—the beautiful Giovanelli.'

'My dear young friend,' said Mrs Walker, taking her hand pleadingly[8], 'don't walk off to the Pincio at this hour to meet a beautiful Italian.'

'Gracious me!' Daisy exclaimed, 'I don't intend to do anything improper[9]. There's an easy way to settle[10] it.' She continued to glance at Winterbourne. 'The Pincio is only a hundred yards distant; and if Mr Winterbourne were as polite as he pretends, he would offer to walk with me!'

Winterbourne's politeness hastened[11] to affirm[12] itself.

They passed downstairs and at the door Winterbourne saw Mrs Miller's carriage waiting, with the courier seated within.

'Goodbye, Eugenio!' cried Daisy; 'I'm going to take a walk.'

1 eloquence [`ɛləkwəns] (n.) 雄辯
2 criticize [`krɪtɪˏsaɪz] (v.) 批評
3 permission [pɚ`mɪʃən] (n.) 允許
4 tremendously [trɪ`mɛndəslɪ] (adv.) 非常
5 personage [`pɝsn̩ɪdʒ] (n.) 大人物
6 proclaim [prə`klem] (v.) 聲明
7 bonnet [`bɑnɪt] (n.) 有帶子的女帽
8 pleadingly [`plidɪŋlɪ] (adv.) 祈求地
9 improper [ɪm`prɑpɚ] (a.) 不恰當的
10 settle [`sɛtl̩] (v.) 解決
11 hasten [`hesn̩] (v.) 加速
12 affirm [ə`fɝm] (v.) 確認

33

As the day was splendid and the traffic of vehicles, walkers, and loungers[1] numerous, the young Americans found their progress much delayed. This fact was highly agreeable to Winterbourne.

The slow moving, idly gazing[2] Roman crowd bestowed[3] much attention upon the extremely pretty young foreign lady who was passing through it upon his arm. His own mission was to consign[4] her to the hands of Mr Giovanelli; but Winterbourne resolved[5] that he would do no such thing.

'Why haven't you been to see me?' asked Daisy. 'You can't get out of that.'

'I have had the honor of telling you that I have only just stepped out of the train.'

'You must have stayed in the train a good while after it stopped!' cried the young girl with her little laugh.

She began to prattle[6] about her own affairs. 'We've got splendid rooms at the hotel. We are going to stay all winter, if we don't die of the fever. It's a great deal nicer than I thought. The society's extremely select. There are all kinds—English, and Germans, and Italians. I think I like the English best. But there are some lovely Americans. I never saw anything so hospitable[7].'

When they had passed the gate of the Pincian Gardens, Miss Miller began to wonder where Mr Giovanelli might be.

'I certainly shall not help you find him,' Winterbourne declared.

'Then I shall find him without you,' cried Miss Daisy.

'You certainly won't leave me!' cried Winterbourne.

She burst into her little laugh. 'Are you afraid you'll get lost—or run over? But there's Giovanelli, leaning against that tree.'

Winterbourne saw, at some distance, a little man standing with folded arms nursing his cane[8]. He had a handsome face, an artfully[9] poised[10] hat, a monocle[11] in one eye, and a nosegay[12] in his buttonhole. Winterbourne looked at him a moment and then said, 'Do you mean to speak to that man?'

'Do I mean to speak to him? Why, you don't suppose I mean to communicate by signs?'

'Please understand, then,' said Winterbourne, 'that I intend to remain with you.'

1 lounger [ˋlaʊndʒɚ] (n.) 閒蕩的人
2 gaze [gez] (v.) 注視
3 bestow [bɪˋsto] (v.) 給與
4 consign [kənˋsaɪn] (v.) 交付給
5 resolve [rɪˋzɑlv] (v.) 決定
6 prattle [ˋprætl̩] (v.) 閒聊
7 hospitable [ˋhɑspɪtəbl̩] (a.) 好客的
8 nurse his cane 小心地拿著他的手杖
9 artfully [ˋɑrtfəlɪ] (adv.) 有技巧地
10 poise [pɔɪz] (v.) 擺出某種姿勢
11 monocle [ˋmɑnəkl̩] (n.) 單片眼鏡
12 nosegay [ˋnozˏge] (n.) 花束；花球

Daisy stopped and looked at him gravely, but with eyes that were prettier than ever. 'I have never allowed a gentleman to dictate[1] to me, or to interfere with anything I do.'

'I think you have made a mistake,' said Winterbourne. 'You should sometimes listen to a gentleman—the right one.'

Daisy began to laugh again. 'I do nothing but listen to gentlemen!' she exclaimed. 'Tell me if Mr Giovanelli is the right one!'

Winterbourne thought him not a bad-looking fellow. But he nevertheless said to Daisy, 'No, he's not the right one.'

Daisy evidently had a natural talent[2] for performing introductions[3]; she mentioned the name of each of her companions to the other. She walked along with one of them on each side of her.

1 dictate [`dɪktet] (v.) 命令
2 talent [`tælənt] (n.) 天份
3 introduction [ˌɪntrə`dʌkʃən] (n.) 介紹
4 heiress [`ɛrɪs] (n.) 女繼承人
5 bargain for 預料到
6 temper [`tɛmpɚ] (n.) 脾氣

(36) Mr Giovanelli, who spoke English very cleverly—Winterbourne afterward learned that he had practiced the language upon a great many American heiresses[4]– spoke a great deal of polite nonsense to her. Giovanelli, of course, had not bargained for[5] a party of three. But he kept his temper[6] in a manner which suggested far-stretching intentions.

'He is not a gentleman,' said the young American; 'he is only a clever imitation of one.'

'Nevertheless,' Winterbourne said to himself, 'a nice girl ought to know!'

And then he came back to the question of whether Daisy was, in fact, a nice girl. Would a nice girl make a rendezvous[7] with a presumably low-lived[8] foreigner? But Daisy continued to present herself as an inscrutable[9] combination of audacity and innocence.

7 rendezvous [ˋrɑndə͵vu] (n.) 約會；會面
8 low-lived [ˋlo͵laɪvd] (a.) 低下的
9 inscrutable [ɪnˋskrutəbḷ] (a.) 不可思議的

THINK

- Why does Winterbourne think that Giovanelli is 'only a clever imitation of a gentleman'?
- What does he think of Daisy and her behavior? Do you agree with him?

She had been walking some quarter of an hour, attended by her two cavaliers[1], when a carriage that had detached[2] itself from the rest drew up[3] beside the path. Winterbourne perceived[4] that his friend Mrs Walker was seated inside and was beckoning[5] to him. Mrs Walker was flushed[6]; she had an excited air.

'It is really too dreadful,' she said. 'That girl must not do this sort of thing. She must not walk here with you two men. Fifty people have noticed her.'

Winterbourne raised his eyebrows. 'I think it's a pity to make too much fuss about it.'

'It's a pity to let the girl ruin herself!'

'She is very innocent,' said Winterbourne.

'She's very crazy!' said Mrs Walker. 'Did you ever see anything so imbecile[7] as her mother? I could not sit still for thinking of it. I ordered the carriage and put on my bonnet, and came here as quickly as possible. Thank Heavens I have found you!'

'What do you propose[8] to do with us?' asked Winterbourne, smiling.

1 cavalier [ˌkævəˋlɪr] (n.) 騎士；護花使者
2 detach [dɪˋtætʃ] (v.) 使分離
3 draw up 停住
4 perceive [pɚˋsiv] (v.) 察覺

'To ask her to get in, to drive her about here for half an hour, so that the world may see she is not running absolutely wild, and then to take her safely home.'

'I don't think it's a very happy thought,' said Winterbourne; 'but you can try.'

Mrs Walker tried. Daisy, on learning that Mrs Walker wished to speak to her, retraced[9] her steps with perfect good grace and with Mr Giovanelli at her side. She declared that she was delighted to have a chance to present this gentleman to Mrs Walker. She immediately achieved the introduction, and declared that she had never in her life seen anything so lovely as Mrs Walker's carriage rug.

'I am glad you admire it,' said this lady, smiling sweetly. 'Will you get in and let me put it over you?' said Mrs Walker.

'That would be charming, but it's so enchanting[10] just as I am!' said Daisy.

'It may be enchanting, dear child, but it is not the custom here,' urged[11] Mrs Walker.

'Well, it ought to be, then!' said Daisy. 'If I didn't walk I should expire[12].'

'You should walk with your mother, dear,' cried the lady, losing patience.

'My mother never walked ten steps in her life. And then,' she added with a laugh, 'I am more than five years old.'

5 beckon [ˋbɛkn̩] (v.) 招手或點頭示意
6 flush [flʌʃ] (v.) 臉紅
7 imbecile [ˋɪmbəsl̩] (a.) 極愚蠢的
8 propose [prəˋpoz] (v.) 計畫；打算
9 retrace [rɪˋtres] (v.) 折回
10 enchanting [ɪnˋtʃæntɪŋ] (a.) 迷人的
11 urge [ɝdʒ] (v.) 催促
12 expire [ɪkˋspaɪr] (v.)〔書〕斷氣；死亡

'You are old enough to be more reasonable. You are old enough, dear Miss Miller, to be talked about.'

Daisy looked at Mrs Walker, smiling intensely. 'Talked about? What do you mean?'

'Come into my carriage, and I will tell you.'

'I don't think I want to know what you mean,' said Daisy presently.

'Should you prefer being thought a very reckless[1] girl?' she demanded.

'Gracious[2]!' exclaimed Daisy. She looked at Mr Giovanelli, then she turned to Winterbourne. There was a little pink flush in her cheek. She was tremendously pretty.

'Does Mr Winterbourne think,' she asked slowly, 'that, to save my reputation[3], I ought to get into the carriage?'

Winterbourne colored; for an instant he hesitated. The truth, for Winterbourne, was that Daisy Miller should take Mrs Walker's advice. He looked at her exquisite[4] prettiness, and then he said, very gently, 'I think you should get into the carriage.'

Daisy gave a violent[5] laugh. 'If this is improper, Mrs Walker,' she pursued, 'then I am all improper, and you must give me up. Goodbye. I hope you'll have a lovely ride!' and she turned away.

Mrs Walker sat looking after her, and there were tears in her eyes. 'Get in here, sir,' she said to Winterbourne.

The young man answered that he felt bound to[6] accompany Miss Miller, whereupon Mrs Walker declared that if he refused her this favor she would never speak to him again.

Winterbourne overtook[7] Daisy and her companion, and told her that Mrs Walker had made a claim upon his society. Daisy shook his hand, hardly looking at him, while Mr Giovanelli bade him farewell[8].

Winterbourne was not in the best possible humor as he took his seat in Mrs Walker's carriage. 'That was not clever of you,' he said candidly[9].

'In such a case,' his companion answered, 'I don't wish to be clever; I wish to be earnest[10]!'

'Well, your earnestness has only offended her. I suspect she meant no harm,' Winterbourne said.

'So I thought a month ago. But she has been going too far.'

'What has she been doing?'

'Everything that is not done here. Flirting with any man she could pick up; sitting in corners with mysterious Italians; dancing all the evening with the same partners; receiving visits at eleven o'clock at night. Her mother goes away when visitors come. I'm told that at their hotel everyone is talking about her.'

'The poor girl's only fault is that she is very uncultivated,' said Winterbourne angrily. And he added a request that she should inform him why she had made him enter her carriage.

'I wished to beg you to cease your relations with Miss Miller—not to flirt with her—to give her no further opportunity to expose[11] herself—to let her alone, in short.'

1 reckless [`rɛklɪs] (a.) 不顧後果的
2 gracious [`greʃəs] (int.) 哎呀；天哪
3 reputation [͵rɛpjə`teʃən] (n.) 名譽
4 exquisite [`ɛkskwɪzɪt] (a.) 精緻的
5 violent [`vaɪələnt] (a.) 猛烈的
6 bound to 一定會做……
7 overtake [͵ovɚ`tek] (v.) 趕上
8 bid farewell 再會
9 candidly [`kændɪdlɪ] (adv.) 率直地
10 earnest [`ɝnɪst] (a.) 認真的
11 expose [ɪk`spoz] (v.) 暴露

he was going to elope
with her. He passed
appening. He could have believed
waited for her in the larg
servants, the foreign tourists, were loun
staring. It w
hould have chosen, but she had decided upon

'I'm afraid I can't do that,' said Winterbourne. 'I like her extremely.'

'All the more reason that you shouldn't help her to make a scandal[1].'

'There shall be nothing scandalous in my attentions to her.'

'I have said what I had on my conscience[2],' Mrs Walker pursued. 'If you wish to rejoin the young lady I will put you down.'

The carriage was traversing that part of the Pincian Garden that overhangs[3] the wall of Rome and overlooks the beautiful Villa Borghese. It is bordered by a large parapet, near which there are several seats. One of the seats was occupied by a gentleman and a lady, towards whom Mrs Walker gave a toss[4] of her head.

Winterbourne asked the coachman[5] to stop and Winterbourne descended[6] from the carriage. Then, while he raised his hat, Mrs Walker drove majestically[7] away. Winterbourne turned his eyes towards Daisy and her cavalier. They evidently saw no one; they were too deeply occupied with each other.

Daisy's companion took her parasol out of her hands and opened it. She came a little nearer, and he held the parasol over her so that both of their heads were hidden from Winterbourne. This young man walked towards the residence of his aunt, Mrs Costello.

1 scandal [ˋskændl̩] (n.) 醜聞
2 conscience [ˋkɑnʃəns] (n.) 良心
3 overhang [ˏovɚˋhæŋ] (v.) 凸出……之上
4 toss [tɔs] (n.) 猛抬
5 coachman [ˋkotʃmən] (n.) 車夫
6 descend [dɪˋsɛnd] (v.) 走下
7 majestically [məˋdʒɛstɪkəlɪ] (adv.) 雄偉地

On the following day, he asked for Mrs Miller at her hotel. This lady and her daughter, however, were not at home.

Mrs Walker's party took place on the evening of the third day, and, in spite of the frigidity[1] of his last interview with the hostess, Winterbourne was among the guests. When he arrived, Daisy Miller was not there, but in a few moments he saw her mother come in alone, very shyly.

'You see, I've come all alone,' said poor Mrs Miller. 'I'm so frightened. It's the first time I've ever been to a party alone. Daisy just pushed me off[2] by myself.

'And does not your daughter intend to favor us with her society?' demanded Mrs Walker impressively.

MRS WALKER

- What is Mrs Walker's attitude to Daisy?

'Well, Daisy's all dressed,' said Mrs Miller. 'But she's got a friend of hers there; that gentleman—the Italian—that she wanted to bring. They've got going[3] at the piano. Mr Giovanelli sings splendidly. But I guess they'll come soon,' concluded Mrs Miller hopefully.

Daisy came after eleven o'clock. She rustled forward in radiant[4] loveliness, smiling and chattering, carrying a large bouquet[5], and attended by Mr Giovanelli. Everyone stopped talking and turned and looked at her. She came straight to Mrs Walker.

'I'm afraid you thought I never was coming, so I sent Mother off to tell you. I wanted to make Mr Giovanelli practice some things before he came; you know he sings beautifully, and I want you to ask him to sing. This is Mr Giovanelli; you know I introduced him to you; he's got the most lovely voice, and he knows the most charming set of songs. I made him go over[6] them this evening on purpose. We had the greatest time at the hotel.' Of all this Daisy delivered[7] herself, looking now at her hostess and now round the room. 'Is there anyone I know?' she asked.

'I think every one knows you!' said Mrs Walker, and she gave a very cursory[8] greeting to Mr Giovanelli.

This gentleman bore himself gallantly[9]. He smiled and bowed and showed his white teeth; he curled his moustaches and rolled his eyes and performed all the proper functions of a handsome Italian at an evening party.

He sang very prettily half a dozen songs, though Mrs Walker declared that she had been unable to find out who asked him. Daisy sat at a distance from the piano, and though she had publicly professed[10] a high admiration for his singing, talked, not inaudibly[11], while it was going on.

'It's a pity these rooms are so small; we can't dance,' she said to Winterbourne.

1 frigidity [frɪˋdʒɪdətɪ] (n.) 冷淡
2 push sb off 打發某人離開
3 get going 使開始實行
4 radiant [ˋredjənt] (a.) 光芒四射的
5 bouquet [buˋke] (n.) 花束
6 go over 重溫；練習
7 deliver [dɪˋlɪvɚ] (v.) 發表
8 cursory [ˋkɝsərɪ] (a.) 忽忙的
9 gallantly [ˋgæləntlɪ] (adv.) 殷勤地
10 profess [prəˋfɛs] (v.) 公開表示
11 inaudibly [ɪnˋɔdəblɪ] (adv.) 聽不見似地

'I am not sorry we can't dance,' Winterbourne answered; 'I don't dance.'

'Of course you don't dance; you're too stiff[1],' said Miss Daisy. 'I hope you enjoyed your drive with Mrs Walker!'

'No. I didn't enjoy it; I preferred walking with you.'

'We paired off[2]: that was much better,' said Daisy. 'But did you ever hear anything so cool as Mrs Walker's wanting me to get into her carriage and drop poor Mr Giovanelli, and under the pretext[3] that it was proper? It would have been most unkind; he had been talking about that walk for ten days.'

'He should not have talked about it at all,' said Winterbourne; 'he would never have proposed[4] to a young lady of this country to walk about the streets with him.'

'About the streets?' cried Daisy with her pretty stare. 'Where, then, would he have proposed to her to walk? Thank goodness, I am not a young lady of this country. The young ladies of this country have a dreadful time of it, so far as I can learn; I don't see why I should change my habits for *them*.'

'I am afraid your habits are those of a flirt,' said Winterbourne gravely.

'Of course they are,' she cried, 'I'm a fearful, frightful flirt! Did you ever hear of a nice girl that was not? But I suppose you will tell me now that I am not a nice girl.'

'You're a very nice girl; but I wish you would flirt with me, and me only,' said Winterbourne.

1 stiff [stɪf] (a.) 僵硬的；呆板的
2 pair off 分成兩批
3 pretext [ˋpritɛkst] (n.) 託辭；藉口
4 propose [prəˋpoz] (v.) 提議

waited for her in the large hall at the hotel, where the cou
servants, the foreign tourists, were lounging about and staring
and decided upon
fanning
or disg
isy turned away from Winter
ng herself. 'Good night,'
sgusted
mething!

'Ah! Thank you—thank you very much; you are the last man I should think of flirting with.'

'If you won't flirt with me, do cease, at least, to flirt with your friend at the piano; they don't understand that sort of thing here.'

'I thought they understood nothing else!' exclaimed Daisy.

'Not in young unmarried women.'

'It seems to me much more proper in young unmarried women than in old married ones,' Daisy declared.

'Well,' said Winterbourne, 'when you deal with[1] the inhabitants[2] of a country you must go by the custom of the place. Flirting is a purely American custom; it doesn't exist here. Though you may be flirting, Mr Giovanelli is not; he means something else.'

'If you want very much to know, we are neither of us flirting; we are too good friends for that.'

Ah!' answered Winterbourne, 'if you are in love with each other, it is another affair.'

FLIRTING

- Winterbourne accuses Daisy of flirting. What is a flirt? What way do they behave?
- Do you think flirting is acceptable or unacceptable?

Daisy immediately got up, blushing visibly. 'Mr Giovanelli, at least,' she said, 'never says such very disagreeable[3] things to me.'

Mr Giovanelli had finished singing. He left the piano and came over to Daisy. 'Won't you come into the other room and have some tea?' he asked.

Daisy turned to Winterbourne, beginning to smile again. 'It has never occurred to Mr Winterbourne to offer me any tea,' she said with her little tormenting[4] manner.

'I have offered you advice,' Winterbourne said.

'I prefer weak tea!' cried Daisy, and she went off with the brilliant Giovanelli.

When Daisy came to say goodbye, Mrs Walker turned her back on her and left her to depart with what grace she might. Winterbourne saw it all. Daisy turned very pale and looked at her mother, but Mrs Miller was unconscious of any violation[5] of the usual social forms.

'Good night, Mrs Walker,' she said; 'we've had a beautiful evening.'

Daisy turned away, with a pale, sad face. Winterbourne saw that she was too shocked and puzzled even for indignation[6]. He on his side was greatly touched.

'That was very cruel,' he said to Mrs Walker.

'She never enters my drawing room again!' replied his hostess.

1 deal with 應付
2 inhabitant [ɪnˋhæbətənt] (n.) 居民
3 disagreeable [ˏdɪsəˋgriəbḷ] (a.) 不愉快的
4 tormenting [ˋtɔrˏmɛntɪŋ] (a.) 令人痛苦的
5 violation [ˏvaɪəˋleʃən] (n.) 違反
6 indignation [ˏɪndɪgˋneʃən] (n.) 憤慨

Since Winterbourne was not going to meet Daisy in Mrs Walker's drawing room, he went as often as possible to Mrs Miller's hotel. The ladies were rarely at home, but when he found them, Giovanelli was always present. Very often he was in the drawing room with Daisy alone. Daisy showed no displeasure at her meeting with Giovanelli being interrupted; she could chatter as freely with two gentlemen as with one.

She seemed to Winterbourne a girl who would never be jealous. With regard to the women who had hitherto[1] interested him, it very often seemed to Winterbourne that he should be afraid of these ladies; he had a pleasant sense that he should never be afraid of Daisy Miller. But she was evidently very much interested in Giovanelli. She looked at him whenever he spoke.

One Sunday afternoon, having gone to St. Peter's with his aunt, Winterbourne saw Daisy strolling about the great church in company with Giovanelli.

He pointed out the young girl and her cavalier to Mrs Costello. This lady looked at them a moment through her eyeglass, and then she said: 'That's what makes you so pensive[2] these days, eh?'

Mrs Costello inspected[3] the young couple again. 'He is very handsome. One easily sees how it is. She thinks him the most elegant man in the world, the finest gentleman. She has never seen anything like him; he is better, even, than the courier. It was the courier probably who introduced him; and if he succeeds in marrying the young lady, the courier will come in for a magnificent[4] commission[5].'

1 hitherto [ˌhɪðɚˋtu] (adv.) 迄今
2 pensive [ˋpɛnsɪv] (a.) 鬱悶的
3 inspect [ɪnˋspɛkt] (v.) 檢查
4 magnificent [mægˋnɪfəsənt] (a.) 極好的
5 commission [kəˋmɪʃən] (n.) 佣金
6 engage [ɪnˋgedʒ] (v.) 訂婚

'I don't believe she thinks of marrying him,' said Winterbourne, 'and I don't believe he hopes to marry her.'

'You can be sure,' said Mrs Costello, 'that she may tell you any moment that she is 'engaged[6]'.'

'I think that is more than Giovanelli expects,' said Winterbourne.

'Who is Giovanelli?'

'The little Italian. I have asked questions about him. He is apparently[7] a perfectly respectable little man. He is evidently immensely[8] charmed with Miss Miller. She must seem to him wonderfully pretty and interesting. I rather doubt that he dreams of marrying her. He has nothing but his handsome face to offer, and there is a wealthy Mr Miller in that mysterious land of dollars. Giovanelli knows that he hasn't a title to offer. If he were only a count or a *marchese*[9]! He must wonder at his luck, at the way they have taken him up[10].'

That day a dozen of the American colonists[11] in Rome came to talk with Mrs Costello, who sat on a little portable[12] stool[13] at the base of one of the great pilasters[14] of Saint Peter's. Between Mrs Costello and her friends, there was a great deal said about poor little Miss Miller's going really 'too far.' Winterbourne was not pleased with what he heard, but when he saw Daisy get into an open cab[15] with her accomplice[16] and roll away through the streets of Rome, he could not deny to himself that she was going very far indeed.

7 apparently [ə`pærəntlɪ] (adv.) 顯然地
8 immensely [ɪ`mɛnslɪ] (adv.) 非常
9 marchese [mɑr`keze] (n.)〔義大利語〕貴族
10 take sb up 接納某人
11 colonist [`kɑlənɪst] (n.) 殖民者
12 portable [`portəbḷ] (a.) 攜帶式的
13 stool [stul] (n.) 凳子；馬桶
14 pilaster [pə`læstɚ] (n.) 壁柱
15 cab [kæb] (n.) 計程車
16 accomplice [ə`kɑmplɪs] (n.) 共犯；幫兇

One day he met a friend in the Corso, a tourist like himself. His friend talked for a moment about the superb portrait of Innocent X by Velasquez, which hangs in one of the cabinets[1] of the Doria Palace, and then said, 'And in the same cabinet, by the way, I had the pleasure of contemplating[2] a picture of a different kind—that pretty American girl whom you pointed out to me last week.'

His friend narrated[3] that the pretty American girl—prettier than ever—was seated with a companion in the secluded[4] nook[5] in which the great papal[6] portrait[7] was enshrined[8].

'Who was her companion?' asked Winterbourne.

'A little Italian with a bouquet in his buttonhole.'

Having assured himself that his informant had seen Daisy and her companion only five minutes before, he jumped into a cab and went to call on Mrs Miller.

'Daisy's gone out somewhere with Mr Giovanelli,' said Mrs Miller. 'It seems as if they couldn't live without each other!' said Mrs Miller. 'Well, he's a real gentleman. I keep telling Daisy she's engaged!'

'And what does Daisy say?'

'Oh, she says she isn't engaged. But I've made Mr Giovanelli promise to tell me, if *she* doesn't. I should want to write to Mr Miller about it—shouldn't you?'

Winterbourne replied that he certainly should. But he felt that Daisy's mamma's way of thinking was so strange a way for a parent to think that he felt it would be hopeless to attempt to put her on her guard.

1 cabinet [ˋkæbənɪt] (n.) 小室
2 contemplate [ˋkɑntɛm͵plet] (v.) 思忖
3 narrate [næˋret] (v.) 講述；
4 secluded [sɪˋkludɪd] (a.) 隱蔽的
5 nook [nʊk] (n.) 角落
6 papal [ˋpepl̩] (a.) 羅馬教皇的
7 portrait [ˋportret] (n.) 肖像
8 enshrine [ɪnˋʃraɪn] (v.) 置於神龕內

Daisy was never at home, and Winterbourne ceased to meet her at the houses of their common acquaintances, because these shrewd[1] people had made up their minds that she was going too far. They ceased to invite her; and they said that they desired to tell observant Europeans that, though Miss Daisy Miller was a young American lady, her behavior was not representative[2] of American girls—was regarded by her compatriots[3] as abnormal[4].

Winterbourne wondered how she felt about all the cold shoulders[5] that were turned towards her. He asked himself whether Daisy's defiance[6] came from the consciousness of innocence, or from her being, essentially[7], a young person of the reckless class. He did not know how far her eccentricities[8] were generic[9], national, and how far they were personal. He had somehow missed her, and now it was too late. She was 'carried away' by Mr Giovanelli.

A few days after his brief interview with her mother, he encountered Daisy in the Palace of the Caesars. She was strolling along the top of one of the great ruins[10]. It seemed to him also that Daisy had never looked so pretty, but this had been an observation[11] of his whenever he met her. Giovanelli was at her side.

'Well,' said Daisy, 'You are always going round by yourself. Can't you get anyone to walk with you?'

'I am not so fortunate,' said Winterbourne, 'as your companion.'

1 shrewd [ʃrud] (a.) 精明的
2 representative [ˌrɛprɪˋzɛntətɪv] (n.) 代表
3 compatriot [kəmˋpetrɪət] (n.) 同胞
4 abnormal [æbˋnɔrml̩] (a.) 不正常的
5 cold shoulder 排擠；冷落

51

Giovanelli, from the first, had treated Winterbourne with distinguished politeness. He carried himself in no degree like a jealous wooer[12]. On this occasion he strolled away from his companion to pick a piece of almond blossom, which he carefully arranged in his buttonhole.

'I know why you say that,' said Daisy, watching Giovanelli. 'Because you think I go round too much with *him*.'

'Every one thinks so—if you care to know,' said Winterbourne.

'Of course I care to know!' Daisy exclaimed seriously. 'But I don't believe it. They are only pretending to be shocked.'

'I think you will find they do care. They will show it unkindly.'

'How unkindly?'

'They will give you the cold shoulder. Do you know what that means?'

Daisy was looking at him intently; she began to color. 'Do you mean as Mrs Walker did the other night?'

'Exactly!' said Winterbourne.

'I shouldn't think you would let people be so unkind!' she said.

'How can I help it?' he asked.

'I should think you would say something.'

'I do say something'; and he paused a moment. 'I say that your mother tells me that she believes you are engaged.'

'Since you have mentioned it,' she said, 'I *am* engaged.'

Winterbourne looked at her.

6 defiance [dɪˋfaɪəns] (n.) 藐視
7 essentially [ɪˋsɛnʃəlɪ] (adv.) 本質上地
8 eccentricity [ˏɛksɛnˋtrɪsətɪ] (n.) 古怪的行為
9 generic [dʒɪˋnɛrɪk] (a.) 一般的
10 ruins [ˋrʊɪns] (n.)〔複〕遺跡
11 observation [ˏɑbzɝˋveʃən] (n.) 觀察；看法
12 wooer [ˋwuɚ] (n.) 追求者

'You don't believe it!' she added.

'Yes, I believe it,' he said.

'Oh, no, you don't!' she answered. 'Well, then—I am not!'

A week afterward Winterbourne went to dine at a beautiful villa [1] on the Caelian Hill. The evening was charming, and he promised himself the satisfaction of walking home beneath the Arch of Constantine and past the vaguely [2] lighted monuments [3] of the Forum [4].

When, on his return from the villa (it was eleven o'clock), Winterbourne approached the Colosseum, it recurred [5] to him that the interior [6], in the pale moonshine, would be well worth a glance, even though its air was known to be unhealthy at night.

1 villa [ˋvɪlə] (n.) 別墅
2 vaguely [ˋveglɪ] (adv.) 模糊地
3 monument [ˋmɑnjəmənt] (n.) 紀念碑
4 forum [ˋforəm] (n.) 古羅馬城鎮的廣場

He walked to one of the empty arches, near which an open carriage was stationed. Then he passed among the shadows of the great structure, and emerged[7] into the clear and silent arena[8]. One half of the gigantic[9] circus was in deep shade; the other was sleeping in the dusk. Winterbourne walked to the middle of the arena, to take a more general glance.

The great cross in the center was covered with shadow. Then he saw that two persons were positioned[10] upon the low steps which formed its base. One of these was a woman, seated; her companion was standing in front of her.

5 recur [rɪˋkɝ] (v.) 重新憶起
6 interior [ɪnˋtɪrɪɚ] (n.) 內部
7 emerge [ɪˋmɝdʒ] (v.) 出現
8 arena [əˋrinə] (n.) 競技場
9 gigantic [dʒaɪˋgæntɪk] (a.) 巨大的
10 position [pəˋzɪʃən] (v.) 定位

Presently the sound of the woman's voice came to him distinctly in the warm night air in the familiar accent of Miss Daisy Miller.

Winterbourne stopped, with a sort of horror, and, it must be added, with a sort of relief. Miss Miller was a young lady whom a gentleman need no longer be at pains to[1] respect. He felt angry with himself that he had bothered so much about the right way of regarding Miss Daisy Miller.

Then, as he was going to advance again, he checked himself. He turned away towards the entrance of the place, but, as he did so, he heard Daisy speak again.

REALISATION

- Think of a time when you suddenly understood or realized that what you had been doing was wrong.
- What was the situation? How did your attitude change?

'Why, it was Mr Winterbourne! He saw me, and he cuts[2] me!'

Winterbourne came forward again and went towards the great cross.

Daisy had got up; Giovanelli lifted his hat.

Winterbourne had now begun to think simply of the craziness, from a sanitary[3] point of view, of a delicate young girl lounging away the evening in this nest of malaria[4].

1 at pains to . . . 盡力去⋯⋯
2 cut [kʌt] (v.) 假裝不看見某人
3 sanitary [ˋsænə͵tɛrɪ] (a.) 衛生上的
4 malaria [məˋlɛrɪə] (n.) 瘧疾
5 brutally [ˋbrutl̩ɪ] (adv.) 野蠻地
6 signorina [͵sɪnjəˋrɪnə] (n.)〔義大利語〕小姐
7 grave [grev] (a.) 重大的
8 indiscretion [͵ɪndɪˋskrɛʃən] (n.) 輕率
9 prudent [ˋprudn̩t] (a.) 審慎的

'How long have you been here?' he asked almost brutally[5].

Daisy, lovely in the flattering moonlight, looked at him a moment. 'All the evening,' she answered, gently. 'I never saw anything so pretty.'

'I am afraid,' said Winterbourne, 'that you will not think Roman fever very pretty. This is the way people catch it. I wonder,' he added, turning to Giovanelli, 'that you, a native Roman, should make such a mistake.'

'Ah,' said the handsome native, 'for myself I am not afraid.'

'Neither am I—for you! I am speaking for this young lady.'

'I told the signorina[6] it was a grave[7] indiscretion[8],' said Giovanelli, 'but when was the signorina ever prudent[9]?'

'I never was sick, and I don't mean to be!' the signorina declared. 'I don't look especially strong, but I'm healthy! I was bound to see the Colosseum by moonlight, and we have had the most beautiful time, haven't we, Mr Giovanelli? If there has been any danger, Eugenio can give me some pills. He has got some splendid pills.'

'I should advise you,' said Winterbourne, 'to drive home as fast as possible and take one!'

'What you say is very wise,' Giovanelli added. 'I will go and make sure the carriage is at hand[1].' And he went forward rapidly.

Daisy followed with Winterbourne. He kept looking at her; she seemed not in the least embarrassed. Daisy chattered about the beauty of the place.

'Well, I *have* seen the Colosseum by moonlight!' she exclaimed. 'That's one good thing.'

Then, noticing Winterbourne's silence, she asked him why he didn't speak. He made no answer; he only began to laugh. They passed under one of the dark archways[2]; Giovanelli was in front of the carriage.

Here Daisy stopped a moment, looking at the young American. '*Did* you believe I was engaged, the other day?' she asked.

'I believe that it makes very little difference whether you are engaged or not!'

He felt the young girl's pretty eyes fixed upon him through the thick gloom[3] of the archway; she was apparently going to answer. But Giovanelli hurried her forward.

'Quick! quick!' he said; 'if we get in by midnight we are quite safe.'

Daisy took her seat in the carriage, and the fortunate Italian placed himself beside her.

'Don't forget Eugenio's pills!' said Winterbourne as he lifted his hat.

1 at hand 在手邊
2 archway [ˋartʃ,we] (n.) 拱廊
3 gloom [glum] (n.) 陰暗

'I don't care,' said Daisy in a little strange tone, 'whether I have Roman fever[1] or not!'

Upon this the cab driver cracked[2] his whip[3], and they rolled away.

Winterbourne mentioned to no one that he had encountered Miss Miller, at midnight, in the Colosseum with a gentleman; but nevertheless, a couple of days later, the fact of her having been there under these circumstances[4] was known to every member of the little American circle, and commented accordingly.

GOSSIP

- People in the story talk a lot *about* Daisy Miller but little *to* her. Think of a time when you heard gossip about someone else. Were you interested? Did you tell the gossip to anyone else?
- What do you think of people who gossip?

They had of course known it at the hotel, and, after Daisy's return, there had been an exchange of remarks between the porter[5] and the cab driver. But the young man was conscious, at the same moment, that it had ceased to be a matter of serious regret to him that the little American flirt should be 'talked about' by low-minded[6] menials[7].

These people, a day or two later, had serious information to give: the little American flirt was alarmingly[8] ill.

1 fever [ˋfivɚ] (n.) 發燒
2 crack [kræk] (v.) 猛擊
3 whip [hwɪp] (n.) 鞭子
4 circumstances [ˋsɝkəm͵stænsɪs] (n.)〔複〕情況

Winterbourne, when the rumor came to him, immediately went to the hotel for more news. He found that two or three charitable[9] friends had preceded[10] him, and that they were being entertained in Mrs Miller's salon[11] by Randolph.

'It's going round at night,' said Randolph—'that's what made her sick. She's always going round at night.'

Mrs Miller was invisible; she was now, at least, giving her daughter the advantage of her society. It was evident that Daisy was dangerously ill.

Winterbourne went often to ask for news of her, and once he saw Mrs Miller, who was perfectly calm.

'Daisy spoke of you the other day,' she said to him. 'Half the time she doesn't know what she's saying, but that time I think she did. She gave me a message she told me to tell you. She told me to tell you that she never was engaged to that handsome Italian. I am sure I am very glad; Mr Giovanelli hasn't been near us since she was taken ill. I thought he was so much of a gentleman; but I don't call that very polite! A lady told me that he was afraid I was angry with him for taking Daisy round at night. Well, so I am, but I suppose he knows I'm a lady, and of course I wouldn't think it correct to show my anger towards him. Anyway, she says she's not engaged. I don't know why she wanted you to know, but she said to me three times, "Remember to tell Mr Winterbourne." And then she told me to ask if you remembered the time you went to that castle in Switzerland.'

5 porter [ˋportɚ] (n.) 腳夫
6 low-minded [ˋloˋmaɪdɪd] (a.) 心地卑劣的
7 menial [ˋminɪəl] (n.) 奴僕
8 alarmingly [əˋlɑrmɪŋlɪ] (adv.) 告急地
9 charitable [ˋtʃærətəbl̩] (a.) 寬厚的
10 precede [priˋsid] (v.) 先於
11 salon [səˋlɑn] (n.) 會客室

But, as Winterbourne had said, it made very little difference. A week after this, the poor girl died; it had been a terrible case of the fever.

Daisy's grave was in the little Protestant[1] cemetery[2], beneath the cypresses[3] and the thick spring flowers. Winterbourne stood there beside it, with a number of other mourners[4], a number larger than the scandal excited by the young lady's career[5] would have led you to expect.

Near him stood Giovanelli. He was very pale: on this occasion he had no flower in his buttonhole; he seemed to wish to say something.

At last he said, 'She was the most beautiful young lady I ever saw, and the friendliest'; and then he added, 'and she was the most innocent.'

1 Protestant [ˋprɑtɪstənt] (a.) 新教的
2 cemetery [ˋsɛməˏtɛrɪ] (n.) 公墓
3 cypress [ˋsaɪprɪs] (n.) 柏；白扁柏
4 mourner [ˋmornɚ] (n.) 送葬者
5 career [kəˋrɪr] (n.) 生涯
6 fatal [ˋfetḷ] (a.) 致命的

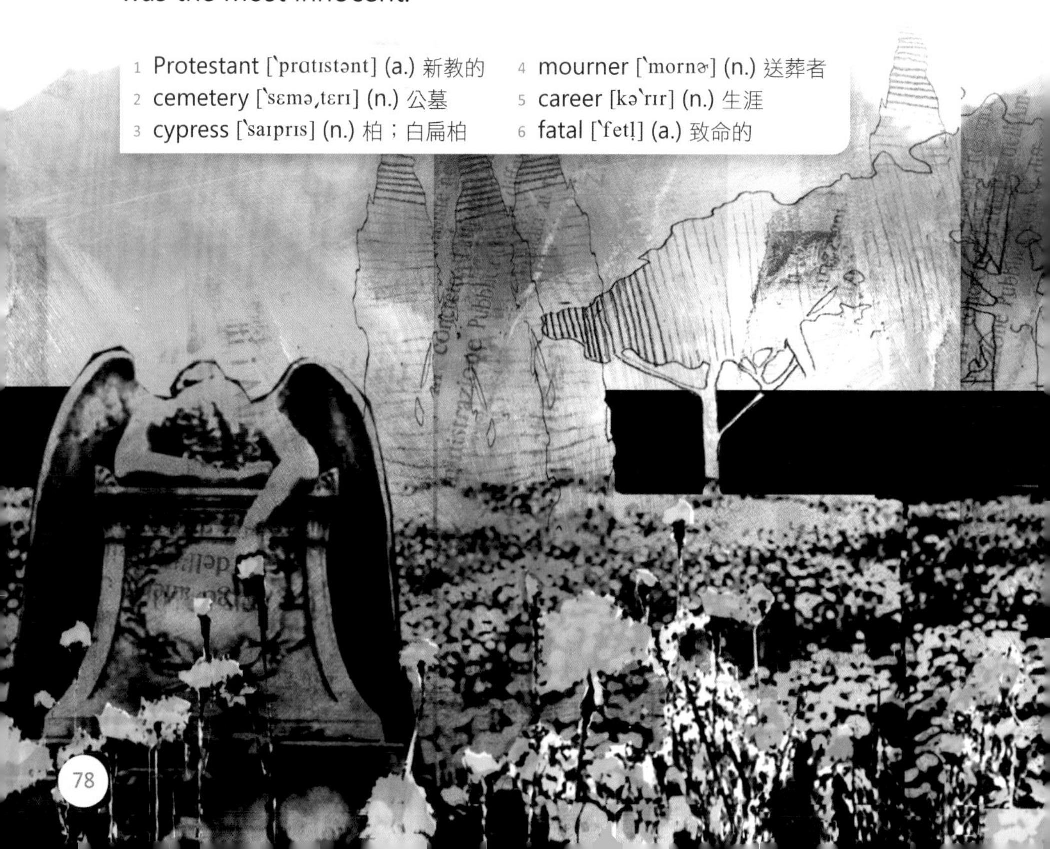

Winterbourne looked at him and repeated his words, 'And the most innocent?'

Winterbourne felt sore and angry. 'Why,' he asked, 'did you take her to that fatal[6] place?'

Mr Giovanelli looked on the ground a moment, and then he said, 'For myself I had no fear; and she wanted to go.'

'That was no reason!' Winterbourne declared.

'If she had lived, I should have got nothing. She would never have married me, I am sure.'

'She would never have married you?'

'For a moment I had hoped so. But no. I am sure.'

When Winterbourne turned away again, Mr Giovanelli, with his light, slow step, had departed.

Winterbourne almost immediately left Rome; but the following summer he again met his aunt, Mrs Costello at Vevey.

In the interval Winterbourne had often thought of Daisy Miller and her mystifying[1] manners. One day he spoke of her to his aunt—said it was on his conscience[2] that he had done her injustice.

'I am sure I don't know,' said Mrs Costello. 'How did your injustice affect[3] her?'

'She sent me a message before her death which I didn't understand at the time; but I have understood it since. She would have appreciated my esteem[4].'

'Is that a modest[5] way,' asked Mrs Costello, 'of saying that she would have reciprocated[6] your affection[7]?'

Winterbourne offered no answer to this question; but he said, 'You were right in that remark that you made last summer. I couldn't help making a mistake. I have lived too long in foreign parts.'

Nevertheless, he went back to live in Geneva, from where the most contradictory[8] accounts of his reasons for staying there continue to come: a report that he is 'studying' hard—an indication[9] that he is much interested in a very clever foreign lady.

1 mystifying [`mɪstə,faɪɪŋ] (a.) 令人困惑的
2 conscience [`kɑnʃəns] (n.) 良心
3 affect [ə`fɛkt] (v.) 影響
4 esteem [ɪs`tim] (n.) 尊敬
5 modest [`mɑdɪst] (a.) 有節制的
6 reciprocate [rɪ`sɪprə,ket] (v.) 報答
7 affection [ə`fɛkʃən] (n.) 情愛
8 contradictory [,kɑntrə`dɪktərɪ] (a.) 矛盾的
9 indication [,ɪndə`keʃən] (n.) 指示

whether I have
whip, and
'I don't care,' said

After Reading

A Comprehension

1 The language used by Henry James is elegant, but old-fashioned. Match the sentences in the first column of the table with the more modern equivalents in the second column.

Henry James' language	Contemporary language
a He was at liberty to wander about.	1 He was about twenty-seven years old.
b He was some seven-and-twenty years of age.	2 I don't want to meet her.
c She was much disposed toward conversation.	3 Lunch is ready.
d I have the honor to inform mademoiselle that luncheon is upon the table.	4 She enjoyed talking to people.
e I must decline the honor of her acquaintance.	5 Why didn't you come to see me?
f I suffer from the liver.	6 He was free to go where he liked.
g You might have come to see me!	7 I have liver problems.

2 Choose the correct answers.

a Winterbourne came to Vevey in order to
- 1 visit an ancient castle.
- 2 stay with his aunt.
- 3 take a break from studying in Geneva.

b When Winterbourne first meets Daisy, he notices that she
- 1 is not embarrassed.
- 2 does not look at him.
- 3 dislikes talking.

c Daisy and Winterbourne are alone during their visit to the castle because
- 1 Daisy wanted to be alone with Winterbourne.
- 2 the custodian was not on duty that day.
- 3 Winterbourne paid the custodian to leave them alone.

d When Daisy asks why Winterbourne didn't contact her as soon as he arrived in Rome, he tells her he
- 1 was sick.
- 2 had to visit his aunt first.
- 3 has just got off the train.

e Mr Giovanelli speaks very good English. How did he learn?
- 1 He attended a language school.
- 2 He practiced his English with many rich American ladies.
- 3 Daisy taught him English.

3 What did they say? Put the following sentences into direct speech:

Example

She told him that they were going to Rome for the winter.
→ *'We are going to Rome for the winter,' she said.*

a Daisy went on to say that she wished Winterbourne would travel with them.

b Winterbourne mentioned to Mrs Costello that he had spent the afternoon at Chillon with Miss Daisy Miller.

c Mrs Walker declared that if he (Winterbourne) refused her this favor she would never speak to him again.

B Characters

4 What's the name of:

a the Miller family's courier?

b Mrs Miller's son?

c Winterbourne's aunt?

d Daisy and Randolph's mother?

e Winterbourne's American friend?

f Daisy's Italian friend?

5 Read these sentences. In each case who is being described?

a 'A tall, handsome man, with a superb moustache, wearing a velvet morning coat and a brilliant watch chain . . .'

→

b 'She was dressed in white muslin, with a hundred frills, and knots of pale-colored ribbon.'

→

c 'He had a handsome face, an artfully poised hat, a monocle in one eye, and a nosegay in his buttonhole.'

→

d She 'was dressed with extreme elegance; she had enormous diamonds in her ears'.

→

e She was 'a widow with a fortune; a person of much distinction'.

→

6 Through which character's eyes do we see the story (the central intelligence)?

7 Here are some adjectives used in the story to describe Daisy and Winterbourne. Which words are used to describe which person? Write the words in the correct boxes.

reckless	guilty	dreadful	nice	puzzled
innocent	stiff	handsome	horrid	pretty
ignorant	perplexed	charming	mean	common
embarrassed	afraid	crazy	uncultivated	

Daisy	Winterbourne

8 Do you like or dislike Winterbourne? Give three reasons for your answer. Share with a partner.

9 What would you ask Daisy? Think of questions and ask and answer with a partner.

10 According to Mrs Walker, 'everyone' is talking about Miss Miller. Write down some things that they may be saying about her.

11 Imagine you are an American living in Rome. Write a letter home describing your impression of Daisy and what she does. Begin your letter like this:

Everyone here is talking about a young lady, an American called Miss Daisy Miller. She is behaving very badly indeed. Yesterday . . .

C Plot and Theme

12 Look at the list of words and expressions that you made before reading the story (Page 8, exercise 1). Were they accurate?

13 Put these events from the story in the correct order.

_____ (a) At her party, Mrs Walker disapproves of Daisy's behavior and turns her back on her.

_____ (b) Daisy dies from the fever and is buried in Rome.

_____ (c) Frederick Winterbourne meets Daisy Miller at a Swiss hotel while visiting his aunt, Mrs Costello.

_____ (d) Daisy tells Winterbourne that she is engaged to Mr Giovanelli.

_____ (e) Daisy falls ill, but delivers a message to Winterbourne that she was never engaged to Giovanelli.

_____ (f) Winterbourne and Daisy visit the Castle of Chillon alone.

_____ (g) Winterbourne meets Daisy and Giovanelli at night at the Colosseum.

14 In the story, what kind of attitude does the American community in Rome have towards Italians? Find comments in the text to support your answer.

15 Write a new ending to the story. Begin from this episode.

> *It was dark, but Winterbourne saw that two people were sitting on the steps. He recognized the woman's voice. It was Daisy Miller . . .*

16 Daisy is described as being 'innocent'. Find examples of her innocence in the text. Share with a partner.

17 In *Daisy Miller* Henry James explores man's inhumanity to man. Find examples of this in the story.

作者簡介

1843 年，亨利・詹姆斯出生於紐約一個富裕的知識分子家庭。他以父親的名字來命名，大亨利・詹姆斯是一位知名的神學家。亨利・詹姆斯自幼便隨家人常常來往美國和歐洲之間，當他居住在歐洲時，由家庭教師來負責他的教育。

詹姆斯的法語、義大利語和德語講得和母語一樣流利，而且他也很喜歡閱讀這些外語的書籍。1864 年，他匿名出版了他的第一部短篇小說《錯誤的悲劇》，從此他就完全獻身於文學創作。

他在寫作生涯中，創作的觸角很廣，出版的書籍和文章包含了各種類型，如小說、短篇故事集、文學批評、遊記、傳記和自傳等。他一生共寫了 22 本小說，其中有兩本在辭世之際尚未完成，創作的故事達 112 篇，此外還寫了不少戲劇和散文。

1876 年，詹姆斯搬到歐洲，永久定居英國，先後住過倫敦和薩西克斯郡的拉伊鎮。第一次世界大戰爆發後，帶給他很大的衝擊。1915 年，他歸化英國籍，宣誓對入籍國家的忠誠，並抗議美國不肯為英國參戰。

詹姆斯於 1916 去世於倫敦，他被許多作家和評論家視為美國的一位偉大作家。他的多部作品曾被改編成電影，叫好又叫座。

本書簡介

《黛絲・米勒》最早刊載於 1878 年六月份和七月份的英國《Cornhill》雜誌上，小說甫刊登即獲熱烈迴響，詹姆斯從此在國際文壇上享有聲譽。他在筆記本上所寫下的一則流言，是這部小說的故事來源。

本書描述一位名叫黛絲・米勒的美麗美國女孩，她與母親和弟弟一起旅遊歐洲的故事。她在途中巧遇了一位叫做溫德柏的美國同胞，她開放親切的態度，深深吸引了溫德柏。然而，她喜歡招蜂引蝶的個性，被其他認識的旅歐美人所不敢苟同。由於對這些社會規範的無知，最後導致了無法挽回的悲劇。

這部中篇小說中所觸及的幾個主題，詹姆斯在後續的作品中，持續都有探討到。這是他對於海外美人行為最早的處理方式。在美國南北戰爭之後的數年間，出現了新的一批商業階級，當時流行帶著小孩旅遊歐洲各地（即所謂的 grand tour），接受教育的洗禮。詹姆斯一方面被美國同胞天真自然的性格所吸引，另一方面也感到比起歐洲各地，他們文化程度較低、見識較狹隘。

作品中還呈現了另一個中心主題：生命並非一定要選擇淋漓盡致的方式不可。在詹姆斯的作品中，故事人物所領悟的是，人們會錯過生命中所一直想追求的東西，並在等待的過程中虛擲人生。

在《黛絲・米勒》的整個篇幅裡，溫德柏花很多心思琢磨黛絲究竟是怎樣的一個人，卻始終理不出個頭緒，也無法明白她在自己的生命中扮演了什麼樣的角色。有些評論家認為，《黛絲・米勒》可視為作者之後的另一部小說《貴婦的肖像》的序曲。

Part I

P. 13

在瑞士一個叫翡費的小鎮上，有一家別致的酒店，就依傍在湛藍的湖邊。湖邊像這樣的酒店鱗次櫛比，其中有一家有別於其他酒店的風格，兼具華麗與典雅，享有盛名。在六月裡，這個地區的美國遊客特別多，到處可見年輕的女子，只見她們或快步走過，或打扮時髦，細薄荷葉邊衣服所發出的窸窣聲時而可聞。在上午時刻，會傳來吵鬧的舞曲音樂；一整天裡，都可以聽到人們高聲交談的聲音。這些景象，在高級的「三冠大酒店」裡時而可見。

兩、三年前，三冠大酒店裡來了一個年輕的美國人，他懶洋洋地坐在酒店的花園裡，看著來來往往的的景象，不知心裡在思索著什麼。

他前天才從日內瓦搭小型蒸汽船過來，探望下榻酒店的姑媽，而他長久以來一直就住在日內瓦。姑媽有習慣性頭痛的毛病，因此待在客房裡，他便趁此一個人出來蹓躂。

P. 14

他約莫二十七歲，朋友說他是在日內瓦「進修」，但也有人說他之所以在日內瓦待這麼久，是因為迷戀上了那裡的一位女子，那是一個年紀比他大的外國女子。關於這位女子的傳聞不少，但卻很少看到她和美國人來往。溫德柏在日內瓦讀書、念大學，年少時在那裡就結交了不少好朋友，而且和很多人都保持聯繫，這大大撫慰了他異鄉人的心情。

得知姑媽身體不適後，他就獨自到鎮上閒逛，等早餐時間再返回。他現在坐在花園的一張小桌子旁，啜著一杯小咖啡，在喝完咖啡後，他點了一根菸。這時，一個年約九歲、十歲的小男孩，沿著走道朝他走過來。男孩臉色蒼白，穿著一件燈籠褲，搭配一雙紅色的長襪，把兩條腿凸顯得更纖細瘦小，脖子上還繫了一條亮紅色的領巾。

男孩的手上拿著一根長長的登山杖，一邊走著，一邊到處戳。花圃、花園裡的凳子、女子的長裙襬，他見到什麼就戳什麼。小男孩走到溫德柏的前面時停下了腳步，用一雙明亮慧黠的眼睛盯著溫德柏瞧。

P.15

「可以給我一塊方糖嗎？」小男孩用粗嘎嘎的聲音小聲問。

溫德柏瞄了一下身旁的茶几，發現還剩幾塊方糖，便說「可以，你就拿一塊吧。不過糖吃多了，對小孩子不好。」

小男孩走向前，仔細地挑了三塊方糖，然後把兩塊方糖塞進寬檔褲的褲袋裡，另一塊則塞進嘴裡，喀喀作響地咬著。

「哇，好硬啊！」男孩用一種很特別的腔調，講出「硬」這個字。

溫德柏立刻認出這種腔調，他可能有榮幸跟小男孩說兩人是同鄉。「小心！別咬壞了牙齒！」溫德柏像個慈祥的父親，對著小男孩說。

「我沒有什麼牙齒，不怕咬壞。我只剩下七顆牙齒。我媽說，我要是再掉牙齒，她就要打我！我會掉牙齒，都是天氣害的！」

溫德柏覺得他講話很趣。「等你把那三塊糖吃完，就等著被媽媽打了。」溫德柏說。

孩提時代

- 回憶一下你的兒童時代，你有什麼特別的習慣會惹爸媽或大人生氣的嗎？大人們都是怎麼說你的？

P.16

「我姊來了！」小男孩喊道。

溫德柏朝走道望去，看到有一個眉目清秀的年輕女郎走過來。女郎一襲白色的細棉洋裝，衣服上綴滿荷葉邊，上面繫著許多淺色的緞帶結。她撐著一把鑲有寬花邊的大陽傘，沒有戴帽子，看起來非常美麗動人。

小男孩這時把手杖拿來撐竿跳，在碎石地上跳來跳去，把沙石都踢了起來。

「藍道夫，你這是在做什麼？」年輕女郎問。

「我在爬阿爾卑斯山！就是往這邊走啊！」小男孩說罷又踢了一下，結果小碎石從溫德柏的耳邊飛過。

年輕女郎盯著弟弟，只說道：「我想你最好安靜一點！」

溫德柏站起身子，緩步走向女郎，隨手把菸扔掉。他彬彬有禮地說：「我和這位小朋友算是有點認識了。」

在日內瓦，除了某些特殊的場合，年輕的男子是不能隨便跟未婚女子攀談的。還好，這裡是翡費，這不是天時地利人和嗎？——在花園裡，一個美麗的美國女子，迎面而來站在你的眼前。

然而，這個美麗的美國女子只瞄了他一眼，便轉過頭對著矮牆外的湖光山色望去。溫德柏心想自己是不是太冒失了，不過他不但不想退縮，反而想更進一步搭訕。他琢磨著找話題，這時女郎又把頭轉向男孩。

P.18

「你那根棍子是哪裡來的？」她問

道。

「我買的！」藍道夫回答。

「你該不會想帶著這根棍子去義大利吧？」

「我是想啊，我要帶著它去義大利！」小男孩說道。

「你們要去義大利嗎？」溫德柏禮貌地問道。

女郎又瞄了他一眼，說道：「是的，先生。」

「你們會經過新普隆嗎？」溫德柏有些尷尬地接著問。

「我不知道，我想大概會經過一座什麼山吧！藍道夫，我們會經過哪座山？」她回答

「我不知道。我不想去義大利，我要回美國。」藍道夫說。

「義大利是一個很美的地方！」溫德柏說。

旅遊

- 你出國旅遊過嗎？
- 你喜歡去過的哪些地方嗎？
- 你出國時會想家嗎？你會想些什麼？

女郎看了看自己的衣服，拉了拉緞帶。看到女郎這副自在的樣子，溫德柏也放鬆了下來。女郎美麗的臉龐沒有絲毫神色的改變，不慍不喜。

P.19

溫德柏跟她講話時，她會別過頭去，一副漫不經心的樣子，但這只是她個人的習慣。溫德柏繼續和她交談，指著那些她不熟悉的景色，她這才慢慢肯多看他幾眼。溫德柏發現她的眼神很直接，看起來很坦誠而且有精神，一雙眼睛長得很漂亮。

溫德柏很懂得欣賞女性的柔美，他喜歡觀察和分析女性美。他覺得，藍道夫少爺的這位姊姊應該是個喜歡賣弄風騷的女子。她當然有自己的特質沒錯，但在她亮麗、甜美、單純的小巧臉蛋上，看不到一點嘲諷的神情。

沒多久，她開始侃侃而談。她告訴溫德柏，她準備和母親、藍道夫一起去羅馬過冬。她說他們是從紐約州來的，「你要是知道那個地方的話。」

溫德柏把她瘦小的弟弟拉到身邊站了一會兒。

「小男孩，跟我說你叫什麼名字？」溫德柏問。

「藍道夫·西·米勒。」男孩口齒清晰地回答，接著大聲說道：「她叫黛絲·米勒，不過這不是真名，她真正的名字叫做安妮·皮·米勒。」

P.20

「你怎麼不問問他叫什麼名字？」小男孩的姊姊指著溫德柏說道。

但藍道夫置之不理，只顧著滔滔不絕地介紹自己的家人：「我爸爸叫伊茲羅·比·米勒，他住在榭內第。他的事業做得很大，很有錢，真的！」

「好了！好了！」米勒小姐喊道。她放下洋傘，看著傘的花邊。

溫德柏放開小男孩，小男孩便又拖著手杖沿著路走開。

「我弟弟不喜歡歐洲，他想回美國。我們一到義大利，我母親就會幫他請一位家庭教師。你想在義大利可以找到好老師嗎？」

「我想應該沒有問題。」溫德柏回答。

「如果找不到，我媽就要幫他找個學校。他要多學點東西，他才九歲，還要上大學的。」

就這樣，米勒小姐繼續說著她的家務事和其他等各種話題。她坐在那裡，兩雙纖纖玉手交疊在膝上，一雙迷人的明眸時而與溫德柏互相對視，時而自顧看著花園，時而望著過往的行人或遠方的景色。

她和溫德柏聊天的樣子，彷彿兩人是多年的舊識，這讓溫德柏感到很舒服。他已經有好多年沒聽過年輕女孩跟他聊這麼多事了。她很文靜，坐姿和神態很安詳迷人，但是她的嘴唇和眼睛始終轉個不停。她的聲音柔細悅耳，講話的語調顯得很熱衷於交際。

P.21

她跟溫德柏說了自己和媽媽、弟弟在歐洲的行程和目的地，還特別列舉下榻過的旅館名字。她說，只要能習慣，那些飯店都是很不錯的，她還說歐洲真是個好地方。

「唯一讓我不喜歡的是這裡的社交圈。」她繼續說：「這裡沒有什麼社交場合，就算有，我也沒見過。你見過嗎？我很喜歡社交活動，而且一直很熱衷，不只是在榭內第，在紐約也是。我每年冬天都會去紐約，在那裡我會參加很多社交活動。我在紐約的朋友比在榭內第多——我指的是男性朋友，當然年輕的女性朋友也很多。」

P.22

她帶著一貫的淡淡微笑，用一雙骨碌碌的眼睛，美麗地看著溫德柏，說道：「我的身邊一向有很多男性朋友。」

她讓可憐的溫德柏感到有趣、困惑，令他傾心不已。他沒有聽過年輕女孩是這樣向別人表白的。他感到自己在日內瓦待太久了，以致於失去了好多東西，不再習慣於美國的方式。

自從他懂事以來，還真沒見過個性這麼鮮明的年輕美國女孩。她的確很迷人，只是過於喜好交際。她真的只是一個紐約州來的美麗女子嗎？那些周旋於男人之間的女子，都是這樣子的嗎？或者，她是那種別有用心、膽大妄為、肆無忌憚的年輕女子？

溫德柏在這件事情上失去了判斷能力，他的理智已經無能為力。黛絲·米勒小姐看起來這麼天真無邪。有人跟他說，美國女孩是最天真的；但也有人說，事實並非如此。

他傾向相信黛絲．米勒小姐是在賣弄風情，是一個風騷的美國美女。他以前不曾跟這種類型的年輕女子打過交道。他在歐洲是認識兩、三個女人很愛賣弄風騷，她們年紀都比黛絲．米勒大，而且為了掩人耳目，都會有名分上的丈夫。她們是很危險、很可怕的女人，跟她們交往，很容易就會惹禍上身。但眼前這個年輕的女子沒有她們那種騷味，她感覺很單純，不過是個喜愛賣弄風情的漂亮美國女孩。

P. 23

「你去過那座古堡嗎？」年輕女孩一邊用陽傘指向西庸古堡的牆垣，一邊問道。

「去過，去過幾次。我猜你們也去過了吧！」溫德柏說。

「還沒，我們還沒去過。我很想去。」

「那裡一路上風景都很美，可以坐車去，也可以搭小汽船去。我想可以安排一下，有人下午時可以幫忙帶藍道夫嗎？」溫德柏說。

米勒小姐看了他一會兒，然後淡淡地說：「我倒是希望你可以陪他。」

溫德柏楞了一下，說道：「我更想陪你去西庸古堡。」

「陪我？」年輕女孩用同樣淡定的神情問。

「陪你母親。」溫德柏恭敬地說。

「那我們是可以安排一下。如果媽媽要帶藍道夫，那我想尤金尼也會留下來陪他們。」

「尤金尼？」年輕男子問。

「尤金尼是我們的侍者，他不喜歡單獨和藍道夫待在一起，不過要是媽媽留下來陪藍道夫，他也會跟著留在旅館，那我們就可以去古堡了。」

P. 24

溫德柏想了一下——「我們」，是指我跟黛絲．米勒兩個人。這樣的行程真令人難以置信。他感到似乎有必要親吻一下黛絲的手，然而，應該是尤金尼，他在這時候出現了。

這個男人高大英挺，留著帥氣的八字鬍，穿著一件絲絨質料的晨袍，袍上繫著一條耀眼的錶鏈。他向米勒小姐走來，眼神銳利地注視著溫德柏。

「喔，尤金尼！」黛絲語氣親切地說。

尤金尼從頭到腳打量了一下溫德柏，然後恭敬地向黛絲鞠躬，説道：「我很榮幸地通知小姐，午餐已經準備好了。」

黛絲緩緩起身，説道：「尤金尼，我跟你説，這次我一定要去那個古堡了。」

「小姐，您是説西庸堡嗎？」尤金尼問：「都安排好了嗎？」他又問了這一句，溫德柏覺得他的語氣很無禮。

年輕女孩把頭轉向溫德柏，臉上泛著微微的紅暈。

「你不會變卦吧？」她問。

「我們如果沒有一起去，我會很失望的。」溫德柏堅決地説道。

「你會住在這間旅館嗎？你真的是美國人？」她接著問。

尤金尼就在那裡站著，用帶著敵意的眼神看著溫德柏。溫德柏覺得他看著黛絲小姐的態度，好像是認為她不應該隨便交朋友。

P. 26

「希望有榮幸向你介紹一個人，她會告訴你我的事。」溫德柏笑著説。他説的人是他的姑媽。

她對他笑了笑，轉身離開。她撐起陽傘，由尤金尼伴著，走回飯店。

溫德柏站在那裡目送著她離去，自言自語地説：好一位美麗佳人。

黛絲・米勒

- 溫德柏覺得黛絲・米勒是怎樣的一個人？

溫德柏承諾説要介紹柯斯提洛姑媽給黛絲小姐，但事實上是不太可能的。他回房間問候姑媽的身體狀況後，便問姑媽是否有注意到酒店裡住了一家美國人——有一位媽媽、女兒和小兒子。

「還有一個侍者，對不對？」柯斯提洛夫人説：「是啊，我有注意到這一家人。我見過他們，也聽説了他們的事，所以會避開他們。」

柯斯提洛夫人是個有錢的寡婦，而且很有社會地位。她有兩個兒子在紐約成家立業，另外一個年輕的兒子現在人在歐洲，住在漢堡市，生活很放縱，很少專程來母親的落腳處探望母親。

P. 27

而她的侄子卻專程從日內瓦到翡費來看她，所以她説，溫德柏比親生兒子還要親。柯斯提洛夫人已經有幾年的時間沒見到溫德柏了，所以這次很高興能有他的陪伴。

溫德柏很快從姑媽的語氣中發現到，黛絲・米勒在社交圈裡的地位並不高。

「您似乎對他們沒有好感？」溫德柏説。

「他們很俗氣。」柯斯提洛夫人答道。

「噢，看來您是不打算理睬他們囉？」溫德柏又問。

「親愛的費德，這我做不到。如果我做得到，我會接納他們，但我辦不到。」

「那位年輕的女孩長得很漂亮。」溫德柏説。

「她當然是長得很漂亮，但就是太俗氣了。她們那種類型的女人，看起來都漂亮。」姑媽繼續說：「她很會打扮，真不明白她們這種品味是哪裡來的。他們對待侍者的樣子太隨便了，好像對待紳士、朋友一樣。如果他跟他們同桌吃飯，我一點也不會驚訝，好像他們從沒有見過這種衣冠楚楚的紳士一樣。也許在那位小姐的心目中，所謂的伯爵也不過如此。他們晚上時，會一起閒坐在花園裡，我想他是有抽菸的。」

溫德柏興致勃勃地聽著，黛絲小姐在他心中的形象愈來愈鮮明，最後浮現出了一個桀敖不馴的形象。

「我不是侍者，但是她很吸引我。」溫德柏說。

P. 28

「你怎麼不早說，」柯斯提洛夫人嚴肅地說：「原來你已經認識她了。」

「我們只是在花園碰過頭，交談了一會兒。我說，我想冒昧地將她介紹給我所敬愛的姑媽。」

「那我可要多謝你囉！」

「我只是要證明一下我是可靠的。」溫德柏說。

「那誰來證明她？」

「噢，你太冷酷了！她是一個很好的女孩。她雖然不是很有教養，但是她很漂亮，總之，她真的很不錯。我會帶她去參觀西庸堡。」溫德柏說。

「我問你，在你們打算一起去城堡前，你們認識了多久？」

「半個小時。」溫德柏笑著說。

「天啊！」柯斯提洛夫人叫了起來，「這女人太可怕了！你在國外待太久了，你一定會惹上麻煩的，你實在太單純了。」

「親愛的姑媽，我沒那麼單純啦。」溫德柏一邊捻著鬍鬚，一邊笑道。

「那你一定是太邪惡了！」

溫德柏繼續捻著鬍鬚，若有所思的樣子。

「那麼，你是不會和這位可憐的小姐見面了，對嗎？」他問。

「你說她要和你一起去西庸堡，這是真的嗎？」

「我想她是當真的。」

P. 29

「那麼，親愛的費德，我還是不要跟她見面好了。我已經老了，可是還好，謝天謝地，我還沒有老到麻木不仁的地步。」柯斯提洛夫人說。

「可是美國的年輕女孩不都是這樣的嗎？」溫德柏疑問著。

柯斯提洛夫人注視溫德柏一會兒。「我倒要看看，我的孫女她們敢不敢這樣！」柯斯提洛夫人嚴厲地說。

他迫不及待想見黛絲，卻不知道該如何開口跟她說，他的姑媽不願意和她見面。當晚，他在花園裡見到黛絲，她在暖暖的星光下漫步。那時已經是晚上十點鐘，黛絲．米勒見到溫德柏時，顯得很高興。

「你一個人一直待在這裡？」他問。

「我本來跟媽媽在一起，後來她走累了。她不喜歡睡覺。她睡不著，睡不到三個小時就醒了。她很神經質。」她回答。

溫德柏跟黛絲散步了一會兒，並沒有見到她的母親。

「我一直在留意你說要介紹給我認識的女士，」黛絲在他身旁繼續說著，「她是你的姑媽。」

她從打掃房間的女服務生的口中，聽過柯斯提洛夫人的事。她很安靜，不和人講話，也不在飯店的餐廳用餐，而且每隔一天就會頭疼發作。

P.30

「我覺得她描述得很有趣，又是頭疼又是什麼的。」黛絲小姐用柔細輕快的聲音快速說道：「我真想認識她，我知道我會喜歡她的。她一定是很清高的人，我也想變成清高的人。其實我和我媽也滿清高的啦，我們也是不會隨便跟別人搭訕的——當然有時候是別人不願意和我們交談，我想這是一樣的道理。不管怎樣，我會很高興認識你姑媽。」

溫德柏感到尷尬。「我姑媽一定會很高興認識你，不過她經常頭疼，恐怕不太方便。」溫德柏說。

藉口

- 你曾經找藉口來推託你不想做的事嗎？你為什麼想找藉口？和夥伴討論一下。

P.31

黛絲透過朦朧的夜色看著溫德柏，「我想她不是每天都在頭疼吧？」黛絲的口氣中帶著同情。

溫德柏沉默了片刻。他不知道如何應對，只好推託說：「她是這麼說的。」

黛絲．米勒停下腳步，站著注視溫德柏。在朦朧的夜色裡，她美麗的容顏依舊清晰可辨；手上的大摺扇開開闔闔。

「她並不想認識我！」黛絲突然開口說：「你為什麼不明說呢？你用不著擔心的。」她微微地笑了一下。

溫德柏從她的聲音中聽到了一些顫抖，讓他有點感動。

「親愛的年輕小姐，我姑媽是誰都不見，因為她身體很不舒服。」他辯解道。

這位年輕的小姐又走動了起來，換了另一種語氣喊道：「你看！我媽媽來了！我猜她還是沒辦法哄藍道夫上床睡覺。」

P.32

遠處出現了一個婦女的身影，身影在黑夜中很模糊，只能看出她緩緩地往這邊走來。

「你母親好像沒有看到你。」溫德柏說。

「她不想走過來，是因為看到你在這裡。」

「喔，那麼我就先告辭了！你母親可能不想看到我跟你走在一起。」溫德柏說。

黛絲正經地看了溫德柏一眼，說道：「只要是男性朋友，我媽媽都不喜歡。只要我跟她介紹男性朋友，她就會大驚小怪，但我還是差不多都會跟她介紹。」

這時他們已經向米勒夫人走過來。當他們走近時，米勒夫人往前移步，倚在花園的欄杆上，背對他們，專注地望著湖面的景色。

「媽媽！」黛絲用果決的聲音喊著。

這位年長的婦女轉過身來。

「這位是溫德柏先生！」黛絲用自然而優雅的態度介紹。

姑媽說黛絲「很俗氣」，但溫德柏發現她在俗氣中有一種嬌貴而優雅的獨特氣質。

她的母親身材瘦小，眼神游移不定，鼻子小小的，有一個寬闊的前額，額頭上覆蓋著捲捲的瀏海。和女兒一樣，米勒夫人也是穿得很講究，耳朵上還戴著很大顆的鑽石。她沒有跟溫德柏打招呼，連看他一眼都沒有。

P.33

「我剛剛在和溫德柏先生聊藍道夫。」黛絲繼續說道。

「喔，是啊，我很榮幸能認識您的公子。」溫德柏說。

「藍道夫是個討厭鬼！」黛絲接著說。

「黛絲．米勒，你不應該這樣說你弟弟的。」米勒夫人說。

「他不肯去古堡，我準備跟溫德柏先生一起去。」黛絲說。

聽到黛絲這樣說，媽媽沒有做出任何反應。溫德柏覺得，她媽媽一定是非常反對這趟行程。但他心想，她媽媽很單純，容易應付，只要說幾句恭維的話，就能安撫下來。

他開口說道：「是的，承蒙您女兒的好意，讓我有機會做她的嚮導，真是萬分榮幸！」

「我們一直想去古堡，但好像就是去不成。」她接著說：「尤其是黛絲，她特別想去逛逛。在英國我們已經參觀幾座古堡。」

「是，英國有很多漂亮的古堡，但這裡的西庸堡也很值得一看。」溫德柏說。

「黛絲要有體力去，就去吧。」米勒夫人說。

「我想她一定會玩得很開心的。」溫德柏問道：「夫人，您不打算一起去嗎？」

P.34

「對啊，能一起去就太好了。」黛絲說道，但她並沒有跟著他走。

「我想你們還是先看看現在是幾點了。」米勒夫人說。

「夫人，現在是十一點。」一個帶有外國腔調的聲音，從他們身邊的黑暗中傳來。

「喂，尤金尼，我要坐船出去！」黛絲說。

尤金尼鞠了躬，說道：「小姐，您要現在十一點鐘坐船出去？」

「我要跟溫德柏先生一起去，就是現在去！」

「告訴她，不能去！」米勒夫人要求侍者說。

「小姐，現在不宜坐船出去。」尤金尼說。

「我想你一定會認為這樣做很不恰當。尤金尼認為什麼事都是不妥當的。」黛絲大聲說。

「小姐打算一個人去嗎？」尤金尼問米勒夫人。

「不是，她要跟這位先生一起去。」米勒夫人回答。

尤金尼看了一下溫德柏，然後莊重地向他彎腰致敬，說道：「小姐，那您就請吧！」

「我還以為你會大驚小怪呢！既然這樣，我就不想去了！我只想看到別人大驚小怪！」黛絲說罷，就又笑了起來。

「藍道夫少爺已經就寢了。」尤金尼緊繃著臉說。

「黛絲，我們現在可以回去了！」米勒夫人說。

P.35

黛絲轉身準備離開溫德柏。她一邊微笑地看著溫德柏，一邊搖著扇子，說道：「晚安。希望你不會失望、厭煩，或是有其他不好的感覺。」

溫德柏握著黛絲伸出的手，看著她答道：「我可困惑了。」

「那希望你不會因此而失眠！」黛絲俏皮地說。在幸運的尤金尼的護送下，兩位女士走回酒店。

溫德柏站在那裡目送他們離去，他感到莫名其妙。

兩天後，他跟黛絲一起去參觀西庸堡。那天他在大酒店的大廳等候，大廳裡到處都是閒晃的侍者、傭人、外國遊客。他不會選在這種地方碰面，但這是黛絲決定的。

黛絲腳步輕盈地走下樓梯，她穿著一套雅緻的外出服，邊走邊扣著長手套，挾著一把陽傘，緊緊地貼著她婀娜多姿的身材。

溫德柏是個富有想像力的人，他看著她的打扮，看著她踩在寬大樓梯上輕快的小步伐，他覺得浪漫的事情就要發生了，彷彿他們正準備私奔似的。

溫德柏帶著黛絲穿過閒晃著的人們面前，人們的目光都集中在黛絲的身上。她一走到溫德柏的身邊，便聊了起來。

P.36

她說她很想搭小汽船去西庸堡，說她

一直就對搭蒸汽船很著迷，因為水面上會有徐徐的微風吹拂，而且可以遇到各種不同的人。

這趟航行並不長，但黛絲在這短短的時間內講了好多事情。人們持續盯著黛絲看，能帶這麼引人矚目的美女出遊，讓溫德柏感到很神氣。他有點擔心黛絲講話太大聲，而且太愛笑了，但這種擔心一下子就煙消雲散了。他坐在那裡，不住地微笑，兩眼落在黛絲的臉龐上，黛絲正口中滔滔不絕地說著自己獨特的想法。他已經開始同意別人說她「俗氣」，但她真的俗氣嗎？或者，他已經習慣了她的俗氣？

P. 37

來到古堡後，黛絲在有拱頂造形的房間中穿梭，衣裙在迴旋梯上窸窣作響。在地牢入口時，她驚叫了一小聲，身子打了個哆嗦，整個人往後退了一下。當溫德柏跟她講解古堡的事時，她伸長了耳朵聆聽。

他們運氣很好，古堡除了管理員之外，沒有其他的遊客。溫德柏已經跟管理員說好了，請他不要催促。溫德柏對管理員施了點小惠，所以管理員也對他們很慷慨，任他們閒逛。

黛絲有很多理由可以唐突地問溫德柏的私人問題，像是他的家庭、經歷、喜好、習慣和抱負。而她自己的喜好、習慣和理想，她可以講得很明確且討喜。

P. 38

黛絲接著說，她希望溫德柏能跟他們一起旅行。溫德柏表示他樂意之至，只可惜他有公務纏身。

「你的意思是？我不相信！」黛絲說。

溫德柏承認自己並非在出差，但他已經跟別人約好，得趕回日內瓦。

「溫德柏先生，我覺得你很可惡。」黛絲說。

「別說得這麼可怕！」溫德柏說。

「我有點想立刻扔下你，一個人回酒店。」在接下來的十分鐘裡，她什麼都沒做，只說他很可惡。

可憐的溫德柏被迷惑了，第一次有年輕女孩對他的行蹤產生這麼大的反應。在這之後，黛絲開始想像在日內瓦的那個神祕女子，她說溫德柏之所以要趕回日內瓦，一定就是為了那個女人。

黛絲·米勒怎麼會知道他在日內瓦有一個令他傾心的女人？溫德柏想不透她是怎麼知道的，但他就是不承認有這樣的女子存在。對他來說，黛絲是一個天真與粗俗的奇異混合體。

P.39

「她是不是不准你離開她超過三天？」黛絲·米勒用酸溜溜的語氣說：「我猜，你只要多待一天，她就會坐船過來找你。」

最後，她告訴他說，如果他願意鄭重允諾，在冬天時也去羅馬，那她就不會再「嘲弄」他。

「要承諾這個並不難。我姑媽已經在羅馬租了過冬的房子，而且要我去羅馬找她。」溫德柏說。

「我不要你為了看你姑媽才去羅馬。我要你專程來羅馬找我。」黛絲說。

溫德柏說他一定會去羅馬找她，黛絲於是不再嘲諷他。溫德柏叫了一輛馬車，兩人就在暮色中踏上歸途回費維。

當天晚上，溫德柏向柯斯提洛夫人提及他下午都跟黛絲待在西庸堡。

「只有她一個人跟你去？」

「就她一個人。」

柯斯提洛夫人嗅一嗅鼻菸瓶，接著大聲說道：「這就是你要我認識的女孩！」

Part II

P.40

溫德柏在遊覽西庸堡後的第二天就返回了日內瓦，然後在一月底時前往羅馬。他的姑媽這時已經在羅馬住了幾個星期，也給溫德柏捎了幾封信。

她在信中說：「去年你在翡費熱絡交往的那些人，已經來到羅馬了，侍者和所有人都過來了。他們認識了一些人，但是那個女孩和幾個三流的義大利人來往密切，惹來了一些閒言閒語。」

溫德柏抵達羅馬後，就應該去查詢米勒夫人的地址，並且去探望黛絲·米勒。

「我們在翡費時有所交往，我應該去拜訪一下他們。」溫德柏對柯斯提洛夫人說。

「如果你認為在翡費或其他地方的那些交往，還有繼續往來的必要，那你就去吧。男人想跟誰交往，就可以跟誰交往。男人就是有這種特權。」

P.41

男性與女性

• 你覺得社會對女性行為的要求和對男性的要求不一樣嗎？

「就談羅馬吧，這裡發生了什麼事？」溫德柏問。

「那個女孩單獨和那些外國朋友出去。至於發生了什麼事，你要自己別處去打聽。她挑了五、六個普普通通的羅馬小白臉到處串門子。她每次去參加宴會，就會帶上一個留著翹翹的八字鬍、很會獻殷勤的男人一起去。

「那她母親呢？」

「這我就不知道了。她們這種人真是要不得啊。」

溫德柏沉思了一會兒，然後說：「她們不懂得人情世故，太單純了，但她們並不差。」

「她們真是俗不可耐！粗俗到無藥可救，算不算是『很差』，這讓哲學家去研究吧。至少她們令人感到厭惡。人生短暫，這樣已經夠受了！」柯斯提洛夫人說。

P.42

聽到黛絲・米勒身邊圍繞著五、六個留著漂亮小鬍鬚的男子時，溫德柏迫不及待想去找她的念頭就退縮了。他所聽到的消息，和他最近盤旋在他心裡頭的畫面格格不入，這讓他很生氣。他想像的畫面是，有一個很漂亮的女孩望著古羅馬式的窗外，一直問著自己溫德柏先生到底什麼時候才會到啊！

溫德柏決定過些時間再去找黛絲，好讓黛絲能夠想起他，於是他便先去拜其他的朋友。

他的其中一位朋友是華克夫人，她是一位美國女士，在日內瓦住過幾個冬天，還讓她的小孩留在日內瓦上學。她是一個教養很好的女士，住在維格那街。溫德柏在一間紅色的小客廳裡見到她，客廳內灑滿了南方的陽光。溫德柏還沒待上十分鐘，就有僕人進來通報說：「米勒夫人到了！」

才一通報，小藍道夫・米勒就走進了客廳。藍道夫在客廳中間停下腳步，站在那裡盯著溫德柏看。緊接著，他美麗的姊姊也走了進來。最後，過了一些時間後，才看到米勒夫人慢條斯理地走來。

「我認識你！」藍道夫說。

「我想你一定學了很多東西！」溫德柏拉住他的手，大聲地說：「你現在學得如何？」

P.44

黛絲正優雅地與女主人寒暄著，當她一聽到溫德柏的聲音，立刻轉過頭來。

「你也在這裡呀！」她說。

「我說過我會來的。」溫德柏笑著回答。

「你應該要來看我的才對啊！」黛絲說。

「我昨天才到的。」溫德柏說。

「我不信。」年輕女孩說道。

溫德柏轉身對米勒夫人笑了笑，表示自己沒說謊，但米勒夫人避開了他的目光。黛絲和女主人聊得很起勁，溫德柏

覺得應該和米勒夫人寒暄幾句。

「我們在翡費分手後，但願您一切都很順心。」他說。

米勒夫人這次終於盯著他看，回答道：「先生，並不是很順心。」

「她消化不良！」藍道夫插著嘴說：「我也消化不良，我爸爸也是，但我最嚴重！」

藍道夫這麼一說，並沒有讓米勒夫人感到尷尬，反而是讓她鬆了一口氣。「我的肝不太好，我想是天氣的緣故。」米勒夫人說。

溫德柏和米勒夫人聊了不少事情，而黛絲也繼續在和女主人交談。溫德柏問米勒夫人對羅馬的看法。

「我只能說我滿失望的。」她答道：「我們聽了很多羅馬的事情，我想我們就是聽太多了，所以跟我們的期待有所落差。」

P. 45

「您再多待一些時間，就會喜歡它了。」溫德柏說。

「我越來越討厭這個地方！」小男孩喊道。

「我們去過許多地方，都比羅馬來得有趣。」母親又說道。

她回應溫德柏的詢問，答道：「蘇黎世就很不錯，它的名氣不及羅馬的一半。」

溫德柏說，他希望黛絲起碼覺得羅馬還不錯。米勒夫人說，黛絲很愛羅馬。

「那是因為她喜歡這裡的社交圈。這裡的社交圈很炫，她認識了很多人。我覺得這裡的人都很善於交際，而且都把她當成自己人看。她還認識了不少紳士。她覺得沒有一個地方能比得上羅馬。當然，一個女孩子能認識這麼多紳士，一定很高興的。」

這時，黛絲將注意力轉到溫德柏身上。「我剛才告訴華克夫人，說你好可惡啊！」年輕女孩說道。

「你有證據嗎？」溫德柏問。

「不是嗎？你在翡費的時候很可惡！」黛絲說：「我要你留下來，你不肯。」

P. 46

「親愛的年輕小姐呀！我大老遠跑來羅馬，就是要你來數落我的嗎？」溫德柏雄辯道。

「這就很難說了！」黛絲一邊撥弄華克夫人的緞帶，一邊說道：「華克夫人，我想告訴您一件事。你知道我是要來參加你的晚宴的。」

「我很高興你這麼說。」

「我有一件很漂亮的衣服。」

「我相信一定很漂亮。」

「但是我想請您允許我——帶一位朋友一起過來。」

「只要是你們的朋友，我都歡迎。」華克夫人一邊說，一邊轉過頭，對著米勒夫人微笑。

「喔，他們不是我的朋友。」黛絲的媽媽說道。

「那是我的一位熟識，他叫做喬萬里先生。」黛絲用清脆的柔細聲音說道，不帶一絲顫抖。

華克夫人沉默了一會兒，然後很快地看了溫德柏一眼，說道：「我很歡迎喬萬里先生。」

「他是義大利人，是我一個很好的朋友，他是世界上長得最帥的男人——只比溫德柏先生差一點。他認識很多義大利人，也很想認識一些美國人。他人非常的聰明，而且很可愛。」

最後確定下來了，這位特別的重要人物將出席華克夫人的晚宴。接著，米勒夫人準備告辭：「我想我們該回旅館了。」

「媽，你們先回館，我還想去走走。」黛絲說。

「她要去和喬萬里先生散步！」藍道夫喊道。

P. 47

「親愛的，你要這時候一個人去嗎？那不安全。」華克夫人說。

黛絲躬身親吻女主人，說：「華克夫人，您人真是好，我不是一個人去，我是要去會見一位朋友。」

「是喬萬里先生嗎？」女主人問。

溫德柏一直注視著黛絲，一聽到女主人這樣問，他的注意力更加集中了。她站在那裡微笑著，梳理著帽子上的緞帶。她瞥了溫德柏一眼，然後不假思索地答道：「是喬萬里先生沒錯，英俊的喬萬里先生！」

女主人拉起黛絲的手，用懇求的語氣說：「我親愛的年輕朋友啊！這種時候不適合走路去蘋丘找義大利帥哥。」

黛絲喊道：「哎呀，我又不是要去做什麼見不得人的事。我有一個解決辦法，」她又看了溫德柏一眼，「蘋丘離這裡才一百公尺遠，溫德柏先生要是真的那麼懂得禮貌的話，他應該就會陪我去！」

溫德柏於是連忙說自己確實很懂禮貌。

他們走下樓梯，看到米勒夫人的馬車正等候在門口處，車子裡坐著侍者。

「再見，尤金尼，我要去散步！」黛絲喊道。

P. 48

這天的天氣很好，路上車水馬龍，街上有很多路人和閒蕩的人。這兩個美國年輕人發現，他們無法走得很快，這讓溫德柏感到很高興。

黛絲挽著溫德柏的手臂穿行而過，那些步調緩慢、到處東張西望的羅馬人，直盯著這位年輕美麗的外國女子瞧。而他的任務，就是把她交到喬萬里先生的手中，但溫德柏決定不做這種事。

「你為什麼不來看我？這你是無法自圓其說的。」黛絲問。

「我剛才已經跟你說過了，我確實是剛下火車不久。」溫德柏回答。

「那你一定是在火車到站後，還在車內待很久！」這位年輕的女孩微笑著說道。

P.49

她開始喋喋不休說起自己的事。「我們旅館的房間真是氣派。我們如果沒有得熱病死掉的話，我們就會在這裡住上一整個冬天。這裡比我想像的還要好，在這裡出入社交圈的，都是精挑細選過的人。各國人都有，有英國人、德國人、義大利人。我最喜歡英國人了，有幾個美國人也很可愛！這是我見過最好客的地方了！」

他們穿過蘋丘公園的大門，米勒小姐開始尋找喬萬里先生的身影。

「我不應該幫你找他的。」溫德柏說。

「那我自己找，不用靠你。」黛絲小姐大聲說道。

「你決不會離開我的。」溫德柏大聲說。

黛絲噗嗤笑了出來。「你是擔心會迷路，還是怕給馬車撞倒？那就是喬萬里先生，靠在樹邊的那一個。」

溫德柏看見就在不遠處，站著一個雙手合抱的小個子，還挾著一根手杖。他的臉蛋很俊秀，帽子刻意斜斜地戴著，一隻眼睛掛著單鏡片的眼鏡，鈕釦孔插著一朵花。溫德柏打量了他一會兒，說道：「你就是要跟那個人談天？」

「我要跟那個人談天？為何這樣問？難道你是要我跟他比手語？」

「那麼只好請你諒解了，我打算一直陪著你，寸步不離。」溫德柏說。

P.50

黛絲停下腳步，嚴肅地看著溫德柏，一雙眼眸顯得更加迷人。「我從不允許男人指揮我，或是干涉我做的任何事。」

「我想你錯了，你有時也該聽男人的話，尤其是值得信賴的男人。」溫德柏說。

黛絲又笑了出來。「我一天到晚都在聽男人說話！你說，喬萬里先生是不是一個值得信賴的男人？」

溫德柏覺得他長得是不賴，但他還是對黛絲說：「不是，他不是一個值得信賴的男人。」

顯然地，黛絲天生就很擅長引介別人認識。她分別向兩個男人互相介紹姓名，並走在他們中間。

P. 51

喬萬里先生的英語講得字正腔圓——溫德柏後來才知道，他的英語是跟很多家財萬貫的美國女人學的。喬萬里向黛絲說了一大堆客套的廢話，他沒有想到會是三個人一起散步，他只好按捺住自己設想了許久的計畫。

「他不是一個紳士，只不過是模仿得很像罷了！」溫德柏說。

溫德柏喃喃自語道：「一個好女孩應該要能分辨真假才對！」

接著，他思考著另一個問題：黛絲是個好女孩嗎？一個好女孩會跟一個下等的外國男人約會嗎？而黛絲，仍是一副既大膽又天真的樣子，讓人摸不透。

P. 52

思索一下

- 為什麼溫德柏會認為喬萬里「只是一個偽裝出來的紳士」？
- 他是怎麼看待黛絲這個人和她的行為舉止的？你同意他的看法嗎？

她在兩位護花使者的陪伴下，走了約一刻鐘的時間，這時有一輛馬車駛出車道，停在小徑上。溫德柏看到華克夫人就坐在車內，伸手向他打招呼。華克夫人臉色潮紅，神情緊張。

「太糟糕了！一個女人家實在不應該這樣子！不應該跟你們兩個男人在這裡一起散步！已經有幾十個人注意到她了。」華克夫人說。

溫德柏揚起眉毛，說：「我很遺憾你們這麼大驚小怪的。」

「這女孩會毀了她自己的！」

「她很單純的！」溫德柏說。

「我看她是瘋了！」華克夫人說：「你見過像她母親那樣愚蠢的人嗎？這件事

我一想到就坐立不安，所以就叫了馬車，戴上帽子就趕過來了！謝天謝地，總算找到你們了！」

「那你打算拿我們怎麼辦？」溫德柏笑著說。

P.53

「叫她上車來，然後載她在這裡兜個半個鐘頭，讓人家看看，說她的行為並沒有太脫軌，然後再把她安全地送回家。」

「我覺得這不是一個好主意，但你可以試試。」溫德柏說。

華克夫人於是照自己的意思做了。黛絲聽說華克夫人有話跟她說，就優雅地轉身走向華克夫人，一旁跟著喬萬里。她說，她感到很榮幸，能有這個機會向華克夫人介紹喬萬里先生。她隨即向他們做介紹，接著稱讚華克夫人的車毯，說這是她見過最漂亮的車毯了。

「你喜歡這毯子，我感到很高興。」華克夫人笑得很甜，「上來吧！這毯子讓你蓋，好不好？」

「坐車是很不錯，可是我現在這樣也很好！」黛絲回答。

「這樣或許很好，不過好孩子呀，這不符合這裡的規矩。」華克夫人催促著說。

「那這裡的規矩應該改了！如果不散散步，我會憋死的！」黛絲說。

「你可以跟你媽媽一起散步！」這位夫人喊道，開始失去了耐心。

「我媽媽這一輩子散步還沒走超過十步的。」黛絲笑著又補上一句：「我已經不是五歲小孩了！」

P.54

「你的年齡是應該懂事了才對！親愛的米勒小姐，你已經到了會讓人閒言閒語的年紀了！」

黛絲滿臉笑容望著華克夫人。「閒言閒語？我聽不懂您的意思？」

「你上馬車，我來跟你解釋。」

「您要告訴我什麼，我並不想知道。」黛絲說話了。

「這麼說，你是喜歡別人叫你野丫頭囉？」華克夫人質問。

「天哪！」黛絲喊道。她先後看了喬萬里和溫德柏一眼，臉上泛起一些些紅暈，看起來更漂亮了。

她慢條斯理地問：「溫德柏先生，你認為呢？為了我的名譽，我是不是應該上車？」

溫德柏頓時紅著臉，不知道如何回答。溫德柏心裡想的，是黛絲應該聽華克夫人的話。他看著她美麗的容顏，溫柔地說：「我想你應該上車。」

黛絲猛然笑了起來，說：「華克夫人，如果您覺得我的行為不成體統，那我就認了，您也就不要再理我了！再見，願您乘車愉快！」說完，黛絲就轉身離去。

華克夫人坐在馬車裡目送他們離去，眼裡含著淚光。「上來吧！先生。」她對溫德柏說。

溫德柏回答說，他應該過去陪米勒小姐。聽他這麼一說，華克夫人表示，如果他不肯上車，那她將永遠不再和他說話。

P. 55

溫德柏追上黛絲和喬萬里，並說明華克夫人說要斷絕來往的事。黛絲握了握他的手，沒有正眼看他，而喬萬里先生則跟他告了辭。

溫德柏坐上華克夫人的馬車，心情並不是很好。「您這麼做並不巧妙。」他坦言道。

「在這種時候我不會去考慮巧妙與否，我只希望自己是真誠的就行了。」華克夫人說。

「不過您的真誠只會讓她反感。我想她並沒有惡意。」溫德柏說。

「我一個月以前也是這麼想的，但現在，她做得太過份了！」

「她做了什麼？」

「在這裡不該做的事，她都做了！她遇到男人就賣弄風騷，和來路不明的義大利男人躲在角落裡；盯住幾個舞伴，跳舞跳一整晚；半夜十一點了還在接待客人。只要客人一進門，她的母親就離開。我聽說，他們旅館裡的所有人都對她議論紛紛。」

「這可憐的女孩，唯一的錯誤就是缺少栽培。」溫德柏氣憤地說。接著他問華克夫人，她叫他上馬車，是不是有什麼事。

「我想請你和米勒小姐斷絕來往，不要再跟她打情罵俏，免得讓她有機會出醜。簡單說，就是不要再理她了！」

P. 57

「這我恐怕做不到，我很喜歡她。」溫德柏說。

「那你就更不應該幫她製造醜聞！」

「我對她的態度，沒有什麼地方是會造成醜聞的！」

「我已經對你說良心話了，如果你還是要去找那位小姐的話，我可以讓你在這裡下車。」華克夫人說。

馬車現在行經蘋丘花園位於羅馬城牆之上的地方，俯瞰著美麗的布吉別墅。那裡圍著一大片護牆，牆邊放了幾張椅子。華克夫人朝牆邊抬頭望過去，只見一對男女坐在椅子上。

溫德柏叫車夫停下車後，便走下馬車。他脫下帽子行禮之際，華克夫人的馬車逕自揚長而去。溫德柏把目光轉向黛絲和她的那位護花使者。他們顯然沒有注意到別人，心思都在彼此的身上。

黛絲的伴侶拿過她手中的陽傘，然後把傘撐開。她緊挨著他，他幫她撐著傘，溫德柏看不到傘下兩個人的頭。溫德柏舉步移動，朝著他姑媽的住處走去。

P. 58

隔天，他去旅館找米勒夫人，結果米勒夫人跟黛絲都不在。

華克夫人的晚宴在第三天晚上舉行，雖然他和女主人上次分別時有些不愉快，但他還是在邀請的名單上。當他來到晚宴上時，並沒有見到黛絲・米勒，但沒多久便見到了米勒夫人一個人羞怯地前來。

「您看，我一個人來了！」可憐的米勒夫人說：「我很害怕，因為這是我第一次單獨一個人來參加晚宴，是黛絲催促我來的。」

「那麼您女兒不願意賞光嗎？」華克夫人很有氣度地問道。

華克夫人

・華克夫人對黛絲・米勒持什麼樣的態度？

「黛絲已經打扮好了，不過家裡來了個訪客，她原本想帶來參加晚宴的，就是那位義大利紳士。他們剛在彈鋼琴，喬萬里先生的歌喉很好，我想他們隨後就會趕過來。」米勒夫人滿懷希望地總結說道。

到了十一點過後，黛絲才來參加晚宴。她打扮得明艷動人，腳步輕快地走著，衣服窸窸窣窣地作響。她笑容滿面地說著話，手上還抱著一大束花，由喬萬里先生陪著前來。眾人看到她來，停止了交談，轉頭直盯著她看。她逕自走向華克夫人。

P. 59

「我擔心您會以為我不來了，所以我就請我媽媽先來告訴您一聲。我想在赴宴之前，先讓喬萬里先生練習一下。他歌喉很好，希望您能請他獻唱。這位就是喬萬里先生，我之前跟您介紹過的。他天生就很會唱歌，唱的都是最動聽的歌曲，我今晚特別要他練習了一下，我們剛剛在旅館時非常的開心。」黛絲在如此講述完之後，看了看女主人，又看看周遭，然後問道：「這裡有我認識的人嗎？」

「我想這裡的人都認識你。」華克夫人回答，並草草地向喬萬里先生打了個招呼。

這位先生表現得很有風度，他微笑地向華克夫人鞠躬，露出潔白的牙齒。他捻一捻小鬍子，轉了轉眼珠，表現了一個義大利帥哥在晚宴上應有的風度。

他唱了五、六首優美的歌，儘管華克夫人說，她搞不懂到底是誰請他開口唱歌的。黛絲坐的位子離鋼琴有段距離，她雖然公開推崇他的歌聲，但是當他在唱歌時，她卻只顧著和別人聊天。

「只可惜這裡太小了，無法跳舞！」黛絲對溫德柏說。

P. 60

「我不覺得可惜，因為我不跳舞。」溫德柏回答。

黛絲說：「你當然不跳舞，你這麼古板！我希望你當時坐上華克夫人的馬車後，旅途愉快！」

「我並不愉快，我比較喜歡跟你一塊散步。」

「我們還是各走各的比較好。華克夫人要我坐上馬車，把可憐的喬萬里先生扔下，還藉口說這樣才合乎規矩，你聽過這麼不近人情的話嗎？這種作法太絕了，他說要我跟他去散步，已經說了十天了」黛絲說。

「他根本就不應該要你去跟他散步的。如果對方是義大利女孩，他就不會要她陪跟他去街上散步。」溫德柏說。

「不去街上散步？那要去哪裡散步？」黛絲瞪著美麗的眼睛喊道：「謝天謝地，我不是義大利女孩！就我現在所看的，這個國家的女孩真是悽慘。我不知道我為什麼要為了『他們』而改變我自己的習慣？」

「我看你的習慣就是喜歡和人打情罵俏。」溫德柏一臉正經地說。

「沒錯，我就是騷。你聽過哪個好女孩不是很騷的？不過我想你現在會說我不是一個好女孩。」她大聲說道。

「你是一個很好的女孩，但是我希望你和我打情罵俏，而且只和我一個人打情罵俏。」溫德柏說。

P. 62

「那我可真感恩了！等男人都死光了，看能不能輪得到你！」

「如果你不想和我打情罵俏，那起碼也不要跟站在鋼琴那邊的那個人調情！這裡的人是不懂的。」

「我看這裡的人什麼都不懂。」黛絲叫道。

「未婚女子是不會打情罵俏的！」

「我倒認為，未婚的年輕人比結婚的年長者，更應該打情罵俏。」

溫德柏說：「跟當地人來往，就應該遵循當地的風俗習慣。跟男人調情，只有在美國才行，在這裡是行不通的。你可能以為你只是在跟男人打情罵俏，但對喬萬里先生可不這麼想，他可能另有所圖。」

「如果你真想知道我跟他的關係，那我就告訴你，我們不是在打情罵俏，我們的交情太好了，不會做那種事。」

溫德柏答道:「如果你們是彼此相愛，那就另當別論了。」

打情罵俏

- 溫德柏指控黛絲在打情罵俏，什麼是打情罵俏呢？那是什麼樣的一種行為舉止？
- 你認為這種行為恰當還是不恰當？

P. 63

黛絲的臉一陣羞紅，立刻站起身來，說道：「最起碼，喬萬里先生不會跟我說這些令人不愉快的事。」

這時，喬萬里先生已經唱完歌。他從鋼琴那邊朝黛絲走過來，問道：「你想去別的房間喝杯茶嗎？」

黛絲轉身向溫德柏，又笑了起來，話中帶刺地說：「溫德柏先生就從來不會說要請我喝杯茶。」

「但我會給你忠告。」溫德柏回答。

「我寧願你給我一杯淡茶。」黛絲說完，就跟才華洋溢的喬萬里離開。

黛絲在告辭時，華克夫人向她別過頭去，讓她自行離去。這一幕被溫德柏看到了。黛絲的臉色變得很難看，只是看著媽媽，但米勒夫人並沒有意識到這種有違一般社交禮儀的舉動。

「晚安，華克夫人，我們今晚玩得很愉快！」米勒夫人說。

黛絲轉身離開，臉色蒼白而傷心。溫德柏看到了她震驚、困惑而又無法生氣的表情，他在一旁感到很不忍心。

「您太殘忍了！」溫德柏對華克夫人說。

「她再也別想踏進我的客廳一步！」華克夫人說。

P. 64

因為在華克夫人的客廳裡不會再見到黛絲，溫德柏就盡可能去米勒夫人下榻的旅館做拜訪。她們母女很少待在旅館裡，而只要她們在，就會看到喬萬里也跟在旁邊，而且常常看到他和黛絲單獨待在客廳裡。當他們的兩人世界被打擾時，黛絲並無慍色。對黛絲而言，不管是和兩個男人聊天，還是和一個男人聊天，她都可以聊得很自在。

在溫德柏的心目中，她是一個不懂得吃醋的女孩。到目前為止，溫德柏對自己所喜歡的女孩會存有恐懼，然而他卻不怕黛絲．米勒，他很喜歡這種感覺。只不過，看得出來黛絲很喜歡喬萬里，每當喬萬里開口講話時，她都會盯著他看。

一個星期天下午，溫德柏陪姑媽去聖彼得教堂時，撞見了黛絲和那位形影不離的喬萬里，他們也在宏偉的教堂旁散步。

溫德柏把黛絲和她的騎士指給姑媽看。姑媽透過單眼鏡片，對著他們看了一會兒，說道：「這就是你近來悶悶不樂的原因，是吧？」

柯斯提洛夫人又打量了他們，說：「他長得很英俊，這也難怪了，她會認為他是世界上最優雅、最英俊的紳士了。她第一次遇到這種男人，他長得至比她家的侍者還帥。搞不好侍者還是他們的媒人！如果他能順利地把她娶到手，侍者也就可以拿到一大筆佣金。」

P. 65

「我不認為她會想嫁給他，也不認為他會想娶她。」溫德柏說。

「可以確定的是，她隨時都可能會告訴你，她訂婚了！」柯斯提洛夫人說。

「我想喬萬里是另有所圖。」溫德柏說。

「喬萬里是誰？」

「就是那個小個子義大利人。我打聽過這個人，看得出來他是一個規矩的人。他顯然是非常愛慕米勒小姐，對他來說，米勒小姐漂亮又有趣，但我不認為他有想過要娶她。他一無所有，有的只是一張小白臉，而在那神祕的美金王國裡，還有一位米勒先生。喬萬里知道自己也沒有貴族的頭銜，他要是個伯爵或侯爵的話，那就太好啦！他一定感到受寵若驚，沒想到他們會這樣抬舉他。」

柯斯提洛夫人坐在聖彼得堡大壁柱下的輕便小凳子上，當天有十餘個住在羅馬的美國人過來跟她攀談。當中有幾個人和她聊到可憐的年輕黛絲種種越軌的行為，溫德柏不喜歡聽這些閒話，但是當他撞見黛絲和夥伴鑽進一輛敞篷馬車，駛過羅馬街道時，他也不得不承認黛絲的行徑的確太踰矩了。

P. 67

這一天，他在考索大街上巧遇一位也是來羅馬觀光的朋友。朋友跟他聊了一會兒，談到一幅掛在多利皇宮展覽室，由委拉斯貴茲所作的教皇英諾森十世肖像畫。朋友接著說道：「對了，就在那個展覽室裡，我還有幸見到另外一幅不同的畫像——就是你上星期指給我看的那位漂亮美國女孩！」

朋友描述說，那位漂亮的美國女孩和同伴坐在一個僻靜的角落裡，那幅教皇的肖像就掛在那裡。女孩看起來比上次看到時還要漂亮。

「是誰陪她的？」溫德柏問。

「一個個子小小的義大利人，鈕釦裡插著花。」

溫德柏在確定朋友是五分鐘前才看到黛絲和那個男人後，隨即跳上馬車，去拜訪米勒夫人。

「黛絲和喬萬里先生一起出門了，他們總是形影不離，還好他算是一個真正的紳士，我老是跟黛絲說她已經私訂終身了。」米勒夫人說。

「那黛絲怎麼說？」

「她說她才沒有。如果『她』就是不肯說，我要喬萬里先生一定要告訴我實情。我應該寫封信告訴米勒先生，你覺得呢？」

溫德柏回答說，這當然是應該的。身為人母，溫德柏覺得黛絲母親的想法很奇怪，看來他不能寄望她媽媽盡到父母的監督之責了。

P. 68

黛絲老是不在家，而溫德柏在他們共同的朋友家裡也不再遇到她，這些精明的朋友們都覺得黛絲的行為太踰矩了。他們不再邀請黛絲，而且表示他們想向觀察敏銳的歐洲人說，黛絲．米勒雖然是一個年輕的美國小姐，但她的行為並不足以代表美國女孩——所有的美國人也都會認為她的言行不合規矩。

看到大家這樣排擠黛絲，溫德柏不知道黛絲會作何感想。他自問著，黛絲之所以會有這種不遜的態度，是因為她知道自己很清白，還是她本性就是一個任性的年輕女子？他無法得知她這些不尋常的行徑，有多少是出自這個年齡層的女孩，有多少是出自民族性，又有多少是來自於她個人的天性。他就是很想她，但他已經錯過了機會，黛絲的心已經被喬萬里先生給搶走了。

在他短暫拜訪黛絲的母親後沒幾天，他又在凱撒宮遇見了黛絲。黛絲正在這一片古蹟上漫步，在他眼裡，黛絲看起來也比之前更漂亮了。事實上，每次遇見她時，他都有這種感覺。她一旁跟著喬萬里。

「每次都看到你一個人，你就不想找人陪你散步嗎？」黛絲說。

「我沒有你的同伴那麼幸運。」溫德柏回答。

P. 69

喬萬里從一開始就對溫德柏特別地客氣，他絲毫沒有表現出情敵的樣子。這時，喬萬里從黛絲的身旁走開，去摘了一支杏花，然後小心翼翼地別在自己的鈕釦孔裡。

「我知道你為什麼這麼說，你認為我太常跟他混在一起了。」黛絲兩眼望著喬萬里說道。

「每個人都會這樣認為——如果你想知道別人的想法的話。」溫德柏回答。

黛絲認真地說：「我當然想知道！但這我不相信，人們只是表面上裝作很震驚罷了。」

「你會發現他們其實是很在乎你的，他們會用一種不客氣的方式表現出來。」

「怎樣的不客氣法？」

「他們會對你很冷淡，你知道這意味著什麼嗎？」

黛絲注視著他，臉頰紅了起來。「你是說，就像華克夫人那天晚上對我的態度一樣？」

「一點也沒錯！」溫德柏說。

「我想你不會讓那些人用那種態度對我。」她說。

「但我又能怎樣？」他說。

「你可以站出來說幾句話！」

「我確實說了！」他停頓了一會兒，又說：「你母親告訴我，她認為你已經

私訂終身了。」

「既然你都提了，那我就告訴你，我是私訂終身了。」她說。

溫德柏盯著她看。

P.70

「你不相信！」她說。

「我相信！」他回答。

「我知道你不相信！」她接著說:「好吧！我沒有訂婚。」

一個星期後，溫德柏去西林山一間美麗的別墅參加晚宴。這晚的夜色很美，他決定走路回家，沿途可以走過康斯坦丁拱門，和月光下隱約可見的古羅馬廣場的紀念碑。

溫德柏從別墅返家時，已經十一點了。他走向羅馬競技場，忽然想到，競技場的內部在朦朧的月色下，一定值得一看，儘管裡面的空氣在晚上時對身體並不好。

P.71

他來到一處無人的拱門下，拱門的旁邊停著一輛敞篷馬車。他穿過這巨大建築物的黑影，來到空曠寂靜的競技場。圓形的大競技場有一半埋在黑暗的陰影中，他走到競技場的中間，以便把整個競技場攬入眼底。

競技場中間的十字架也隱沒在黑暗中，這時，他看見十字架基座的石階上有兩個身影，其中一個是女性，坐在石階上，而另一個人則站在她的前面。

P.72

這時，女子的聲音從夜晚溫暖的空氣中，清晰地傳入他的耳裡，這是熟悉的黛絲．米勒小姐的聲音。

溫德柏停下腳步，一方面嚇了一跳，另一方面又鬆了口氣。黛絲．米勒這位年輕的女士，是不需要男士費盡心思去表示尊重的。他對自己感到氣惱，因為他一直以來都在費心思考著到底要用什麼樣的眼光來看待黛絲．米勒小姐。

之後正當他打算再往前走時，他克制了自己。他轉身走向廣場的出口，這時，又傳來了黛絲說話的聲音。

省悟

- 你曾經突然領悟或了解到自己錯了嗎？
- 那是什麼事？你的想法怎麼會突然改變的？

「看，是溫德柏先生，他看到了我，卻故意不理我！」

溫德柏又向前走去，走向大十字架。

黛絲已經站起身來，喬萬里舉起帽子表示禮貌。

溫德柏這時只想到她的健康問題，一個身體嬌弱的年輕女孩子，在這種有瘧疾的地方消磨了一個晚上，真是瘋了。

P.73

「你在這裡待多久了？」他問話的口氣有點粗魯。

在美麗的月色下，黛絲顯得楚楚動人。她看了他一會兒，輕柔地回答說：「我們已經待一個晚上了，我沒見過這麼美的地方。」

「你該不會認為羅馬的瘧疾很美吧！這樣很容易染上瘧疾的。」他轉向喬萬里，說：「我不懂，你是本地人，怎麼會犯這種錯誤！」

「我自己是不怕的。」這位英俊的本地人說。

「我也不怕，我不是在擔心你，我是擔心這位年輕的小姐。」

「我告訴她，這樣不太好，但她曾幾何時謹慎過呢？」喬萬里說。

「我沒生過病，我不會生病的！我看起來雖然不是很強壯，但我的身體很好！我一定要看看月光下的競技場，我們在這裡玩得很開心，對不對，喬萬里先生？要是真有什麼危險的話，尤金尼可以給我吃些藥。他有一些很有效的藥。」黛絲說。

P.74

「那我建議你趕緊坐上馬車回去吃藥！」溫德柏說。

「你說得沒錯！我去看看，叫馬車準備好！」喬萬里說完，便快步向前走去。

黛絲和溫德柏在後面跟著。溫德柏目不轉睛地盯著她看，而她似乎一點也不會感到彆扭。黛絲不停地說著這地方有多美。

「我終於看到月光下的競技場了！」她歡呼地叫著：「太棒了！」

這時，她留意到溫德柏都不講話，就問他為什麼不說話。他沒有回答，只是笑了笑。他們通過黑暗的拱門，喬萬里就站在馬車的前面。

黛絲停下腳步，望著年輕的美國人，問道：「你那天真相信我私訂終身了嗎？」

「我想，你私訂終身與否，並沒有什麼差別！」

他感到黛絲美麗的眼睛，正透過拱門下重重的黑暗凝視著他。她顯然想回答他一些什麼，可是喬萬里催促著她。

「快上車！如果能在午夜以前趕回家，我們就會平安無事的。」喬萬里說。

黛絲坐上馬車裡，這位幸運的義大利人在她旁邊跟著坐下。

「別忘了跟尤金尼討些藥吃！」溫德柏一邊說，一邊脫帽揮別。

P.76

「我才不在乎！」黛絲用怪怪的語調說：「我得不得瘧疾，有什麼關係？」

她話一說完，車夫揚起馬鞭用力一揮，馬車便揚長而去。

溫德柏沒有跟任何人提及他半夜在競技場看到米勒小姐和男人在一起的事，可是沒過幾天，在小小的美國人圈子裡，大家都知道了這種事，而且議論紛紛。

流言蜚語

- 在這個故事裡，人們對黛絲・米勒議論紛紛，卻很少和她講話。你曾經聽過別人在講閒話嗎？你有興趣聽嗎？你會跟別人說流言蜚語嗎？
- 你覺得喜歡講別人八卦的人，是怎樣的人？

事情一定是在旅館那裡傳開的。黛絲回旅館後，車夫和門房就開始互相耳語了起來。但是溫德柏也瞭解，這位喜歡賣弄風情的女孩，即使被下人這樣閒言閒語，他也不會感到太過遺憾。

一、兩天後，這些人更流傳著令人震驚的消息：那位喜歡賣弄風騷的美國女孩，病情告急。

P.77

溫德柏聽到這個消息後，立即趕到旅館去打聽。他發現兩、三個好心的朋友已經先到一步，而藍道夫正在米勒夫人的客廳裡招呼他們。

藍道夫說：「都是因為晚上到處亂跑，才會得到這種病。她老是喜歡晚上出門。」

米勒夫人始終沒有露臉，而此時此刻，她的社交圈也算是對她女兒不錯了。看樣子，黛絲的病情一定很嚴重。

溫德柏經常去探視黛絲的病情，有一次，他見到了米勒夫人，而米勒夫人表現得很鎮定。

她說：「黛絲那天有提到你，她有一

半的時間都在譫妄，可是在提到你時，意識是清醒的。她要我轉告你，她壓根就沒和那位義大利帥哥私訂終身過。我很高興聽到她這麼講，自從她病倒了之後，喬萬里先生就沒有出現過，我還以為他是個紳士，他那樣做實在是太失禮了！有一位女士跟我說，他是怕我對他發脾氣，怪他晚上帶黛絲到處亂跑。我當然是生氣，可是他應該知道，我是有身分地位的人，當然不會去指責他的。不管怎麼說，黛絲說她沒有私訂終身過。我不知道她為什麼要你明白這件事，她跟我說了三次，要我『務必轉告溫德柏先生』。然後她還要我問你，說你是不是還記得你們一起去瑞士那座城堡的事。」

P.78

然而，就如溫德柏所講的，事情已經沒有什麼差別了！一個星期之後，可憐的女孩香消玉殞了，死於嚴重的瘧疾。

黛絲葬在一個小小的新教墓園裡，就葬在柏樹和繁密的春花之下。溫德柏站在墓前，旁邊還有幾位送葬的朋友，人數比預期的還多。她生前引人議論紛紛，死後還有這麼多人來為她送行。

喬萬里就站在他附近，他臉色很蒼白，這一次他的鈕釦孔裡沒有插著花，他好像有話要說似的。

最後他終於開口說：「她是我見過最美麗、也是最親切的年輕女孩了。」之後他又加上一句：「也是最純真的女孩。」

P.79

溫德柏看一下他，自言自語地重複道：「最純真？」

溫德柏感到一陣心痛與憤怒，問道：「那你為什麼還要帶她去那種要命的地方？」

喬萬里先生看了地面一會兒，說道：「我自己是不怕，是她堅持要去的。」

「這不是理由！」溫德柏說。

「如果她還活著，我也是一無所有。我很清楚，她是不可能和我結婚的！」

「她不可能和你結婚？」

「我是曾經想和她結婚，但那是不可能的，這我知道。」

當溫德柏再次轉身，發現喬萬里已經緩步離去。

P. 80

溫德柏差不多隨即就離開了羅馬。第二年，他又去翡費拜訪姑媽柯斯提洛夫人。

這期間，溫德柏常常想起．米勒黛絲和她令人迷惑不解的行徑。有一天，他和姑媽談起黛絲，他說他感到良心不安，覺得他對黛絲不公平。

「這我就不明白了，就算你對她公不公平，對她又有什麼影響？」柯斯提洛夫人問。

「她臨死前曾捎話給我，當時我還不能瞭解，後來我懂了，她很感激我對她的尊重。」

「這是她想回報你的感情的委婉說法嗎？」柯斯提洛夫人問。

溫德柏沒有回答，只是說道：「您去年夏天說的話沒有錯，我是要鑄成大錯的，我在國外確實是住太久了。」

儘管這麼說，他還是返回日內瓦定居了。至於他為什麼要在日內瓦落腳，又繼續流傳著互相矛盾的說法：據說他是在求學，但這其實就是在說，他迷戀上了一位聰明的外國女子。

ANSWER KEY

After Reading

Page 82

1
a) 6
b) 1
c) 4
d) 3
e) 2
f) 7
g) 5

Page 84

2
a) 2
b) 1
c) 3
d) 3
e) 2

Page 85

3 (Possible answers)
a) "I wish you would travel with us," continued Daisy.
b) "I spent the afternoon at Chillon with Miss Daisy Miller," said Winterbourne.
c) "I will never speak to you again if you refuse me this favor!" said Mrs Walker.

4
a) Eugenio
b) Randolph Miller
c) Mrs Costello
d) Mrs Miller
e) Mrs Walker
f) Mr Giovanelli

Page 86

5
a) Eugenio
b) Daisy Miller
c) Mr Giovanelli
d) Mrs Miller
e) Mrs Costello

6 Winterbourne's

Page 87

7

Daisy	Winterbourne
reckless	*guilty*
dreadful	*puzzled*
nice	*stiff*
innocent	*handsome*
pretty	*horrid*
ignorant	*perplexed*
charming	*mean*
common	*afraid*
crazy	*embarrassed*
uncultivated	

Page 88

13
a) 3
b) 7
c) 1
d) 4
e) 6
f) 2
g) 5

國家圖書館出版品預行編目資料

黛絲・米勒 / Janet Olearski 著 ; 安卡斯 譯 . 一初版 . 一 [臺北市] : 寂天文化， 2012.7 面； 公分 .

中英對照

ISBN 978-986-318-019-7 (25K 平裝附光碟片)

1. 英語 2. 讀本

805.18 101011886

■原著 _ Henry James ■改寫 _ Janet Olearski

■譯者 _ 安卡斯 ■校對 _ 陳慧莉 ■封面設計 _ 蔡怡柔

■主編 _ 黃鈺云 ■製程管理 _ 蔡智堯

■出版者 _ 寂天文化事業股份有限公司 ■電話 _ 02-2365-9739 ■傳真 _ 02-2365-9835

■網址 _ www.icosmos.com.tw ■讀者服務 _ onlineservice@icosmos.com.tw

■出版日期 _ 2012年7月 初版一刷（250101）

■郵撥帳號 _ 1998620-0 寂天文化事業股份有限公司

■訂購金額600（含）元以上郵資免費 ■訂購金額600元以下者，請外加郵資60元

■若有破損，請寄回更換